*Suddenly* as if he took up more space than one man should.

Taller than she'd thought he'd be, broad shouldered in an immaculately cut dark suit, black hair and a handsome, handsome face. He was hot. So hot she could not help but stare. And then when he got closer, stare some more.

"Marissa Gracey?" he said in a deep, clear voice. "Oliver Pierce." He held out his hand for her to shake.

All Marissa could do was nod before he continued. "Right on time. Good."

It was just as well he hadn't expected a reply because she was suddenly without a voice. She felt the color flush hot on her cheeks then rush back to pale.

She knew this man.

Only he'd called himself Oliver Hughes back then. Back when they'd both been teenagers and she'd thought him the most insufferable, arrogant, rude person she had ever met. Marissa's thoughts flashed back to when she'd been fourteen years old and deeply, desperately and very secretly in love with a sixteen-year-old boy she'd known as Oliver Hughes.

Dear Reader,

Do you believe in love at first sight? Does it seem possible? I can vouch for love at first sight. I remember the very first time I met my husband. A friend introduced us, and it was instant attraction. Three days later we decided to spend our lives together. Ten months later we married. We recently celebrated our thirty-fifth anniversary. Love at first sight worked!

What about Marissa and Oliver, the heroine and hero of *The Tycoon's Christmas Dating Deal*? There's instant, powerful attraction between the lovely event planner and the movie-star handsome hotel tycoon. Both have heartbreak in their pasts, and I loved bringing these wonderful people together. But there are complications...not the least of which is the secret Marissa is keeping from Oliver.

*The Tycoon's Christmas Dating Deal* is a Christmas story set in a fabulous country house hotel—Oliver's ancestral home. Marissa's brief is to create the best Christmas celebrations ever at Longfield Manor. Think luxury, beautiful rooms, gorgeous gardens, Christmas trees and snow—lots of glorious snow.

I hope you enjoy following Marissa and Oliver's journey to a once-in-a-lifetime forever love.

Warm regards,

*Kandy*

# THE TYCOON'S CHRISTMAS DATING DEAL

## KANDY SHEPHERD

**Harlequin**

**ROMANCE**

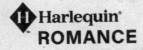

# Harlequin®
# ROMANCE

Recycling programs for this product may not exist in your area.

ISBN-13: 978-1-335-21615-1

The Tycoon's Christmas Dating Deal

Copyright © 2024 by Kandy Shepherd

Harlequin Enterprises ULC
22 Adelaide St. West, 41st Floor
Toronto, Ontario M5H 4E3, Canada
www.Harlequin.com

Printed in U.S.A.

**Kandy Shepherd** swapped a career as a magazine editor for a life writing romance. She lives on a small farm in the Blue Mountains near Sydney, Australia, with her husband, daughter and lots of pets. She believes in love at first sight and real-life romance—they worked for her! Kandy loves to hear from her readers. Visit her at kandyshepherd.com.

To my longtime friend and fellow author
Cathleen Ross, for being my first reader.
Thank you!

# CHAPTER ONE

Marissa Gracey hated Christmas. As she strode along Kensington High Street in London, two weeks before December the twenty-fifth, she felt assaulted by Christmas cheer. Everything that could possibly be festooned with lights twinkled garishly in the evening gloom—trees, lampposts, storefronts, even a bus stop shelter, which should surely be illegal. Alcoves and shop windows were stuffed with overdecorated Christmas trees. Clashing Christmas carols, loud and shmaltzy, blared out from doorways.

*Fa-la-la-la-la, la-la-la-la*, indeed, she thought with a deep scowl.

Every step she took she was exhorted to feel merry, happy and jolly. But she didn't feel any of that. Not even a glimmering of merriment. Not anymore.

Marissa knew that behind her back she was called a Scrooge and a Grinch. That hurt. But she couldn't share the details of why she no longer celebrated the season. Because she couldn't bear to be reminded of the heartbreak and pain. Bad things had happened to her at Christmas. The car crash five years ago that had killed her parents. Her brother's departure to the other side of the world. The out-of-the-blue firing from her dream job on Christmas Eve. And the most recent—the betrayal of her boyfriend, whom she'd last year caught kissing another woman under the mistletoe. Disasters that had rocked her world at Christmastime. She'd begun to believe she was jinxed. If she allowed herself to enjoy Christmas, who knew what other horrible thing might happen?

There was excited chatter among her fellow pedestrians when a scattering of fat snowflakes drifted down from the sky. She looked up but resisted the temptation to try to catch a snowflake on her tongue, like she'd done when she was a child. Back then, Christmas had seemed magical.

A man started to sing, very off-key, that he was dreaming of a white Christmas.

*Huh*, Marissa thought, *a sleety, slippery Christmas more likely*.

London rarely had decent snow in December. Thankfully, she would be out of here in five days, flying to a small island off the east coast of Bali, where Christmas wasn't part of the culture. By the time she got back, the decorations and all the painful reminders they brought with them would be taken down.

She detoured into the supermarket—more detestable carols were piped through the store—in search of a ready meal for her dinner. She lived alone in her flat in West Kensington and often couldn't be bothered to cook for herself. She studiously avoided the displays of mince pies. Her father had loved the small, sweet, spiced fruit pastries, traditionally only available at Christmastime. His Christmas Eve ritual had been to eat an entire packet of six mince pies—with lashings of custard and ice cream—in one sitting, egged on by a laughing Marissa and her brother while her mother pretended to be shocked. Until that Christmas Eve five years ago when the mince pies had remained uneaten in the kitchen while her dad lay still on a hospital bed, attached to tubes and monitors that hadn't saved his life. It still hurt to see mince pies and remember his joy in them.

When her friend Caity Johnston called on her mobile phone, Marissa had to swallow hard against the lump of remembered grief that threatened to choke her.

'Everything okay?' she asked, when she was in control of her voice. Caity was expecting twins, due in the middle of January.

'Actually, no,' Caity said. Her friend's voice sounded anxious, frayed at the edges.

Terror for her friend shot through Marissa. 'The babies?'

'Okay.'

Marissa breathed a sigh of relief.

'But I have to go to hospital and stay in bed until the due date. Or whenever the consultant decides it's time for the babies to be born.' Caity's voice rose.

'Oh, Caity. What can I do to help?'

'Could you… Could you get over here now?'

'On my way,' Marissa said as she hailed a black cab.

Mentally, she urged the driver to hurry. It seemed the longest trip ever to the west London suburb of Ealing. She'd normally go by the Underground, it was nearly as fast and a tenth of the cab fare, but there was an edge of fear to Caity's voice that had truly scared Marissa. Two years ago, her friend had miscarried at twenty weeks. Marissa would do anything she could to help her carry her twins to term.

When she arrived at Caity's house twenty minutes later, a terrace in a street of terraces that she and her husband, Tom, had painstakingly remodelled, her friend was waiting for her. Her face was pale, and she was anxiously wringing her hands. Caity was tiny and slight except for her enormous bump. Marissa noticed a bulging overnight bag in the hallway.

She hugged her friend gently. 'What's happened?'

'I'm sure I mentioned before that the twins share the same placenta. That can be dangerous so the doctors want me under observation. My bump and I will be hooked up to monitors for the next few weeks.'

'Oh, no!' Marissa exclaimed, and then immediately backpedalled. She didn't want her alarmed reaction to add further to Caity's obvious fears. 'I mean, that's good they're being vigilant.'

'It's unlikely I'll leave hospital until the babies are born.'

'You'll be in good hands. Do you want me to go with you to the hospital, to get you settled?'

Caity shook her head. 'No. Tom's taken time off work. He's out getting the car from where it's parked. But there is something you could do to help me.'

'Anything,' Marissa said.

She and Caity had started work as interns in

a public relations firm back when they'd been fresh out of uni. They'd both specialised in event planning until there was a big downturn in business and they were both let go from the jobs they'd loved—just before Christmas. Caity had bounced back quickly and started her own company, while Marissa freelanced for her and other marketing companies in the city, trying to find the place where she best fit. Now, at age thirty, Marissa wasn't sure about what direction she wanted her career to take. She only knew that she didn't want to tie herself down to the one employer. Not yet. Experience had taught her that it was too dangerous to put her fate in someone else's hands.

'I hate to ask you this, as I know you're not a fan of Christmas…' Caity began, tentatively, not meeting Marissa's eyes.

Marissa's heart sank. Caity was one of the few people who understood her aversion to the festive season. So why was she bringing it up now?

She narrowed her eyes. 'Er, yes?' she said.

Caity's words spilled out. 'There's this Christmas event I've been working on. Longfield Manor is a beautiful country house hotel in Dorset. Family run. Christmas is a huge deal for them. People come from around the country—

even the world—year after year to celebrate the holiday season there, and this year is the first time the family has brought in an event planner to organise the festivities. And now, two weeks out from the most important commission of my career, I have to go into hospital.'

*To save her babies' lives.*

The words were unspoken but Marissa heard them.

'And you want me to step in?' she said, trying to keep the dismay from her voice. 'Caity, you know how I feel—'

'About Christmas? I know. And I wouldn't ask you if I had any choice. The grandson of the hotel owners, Oliver Pierce, is the CEO of The Pierce Group of hotels.'

'The most exclusive, fashionable hotels in London. I know of them.' Although as she'd need to take out a mortgage to buy a cocktail there, Marissa had never been to one.

'I've done some work for him in the past and it went really well, and I *need* to keep The Pierce Group as a client. Oliver Pierce himself asked me to help with the Longfield Manor Christmas. Marissa, this job could change the entire trajectory for my company. It's my big break. I can't risk losing his business.'

'Couldn't someone else—?'

'He's a very discerning man,' Caity said, cutting her off. 'I couldn't trust anyone else but you to take over this particular job.'

'Surely there must be another planner who——?'

'You're the only person who is good enough and I know you would never let me down,' Caity said. 'Or try to steal my client.'

That was Caity all right. A shrewd businesswoman whose boutique event planning business was very successful, yet not established enough to be able to risk losing an important client. Marissa knew how vital the personal relationship between client and planner could be. And satisfied clients led to recommendations and further business. If Caity couldn't trust anyone else but her—her best friend—to run this job, Marissa could put up no further resistance.

'Please,' Caity pleaded. 'I… I'm begging you. You know how much I want these babies.' Her voice caught. 'And I can't do the job from a hospital bed.'

Marissa took a deep breath. 'Of course not. Nor should you. All your energies should be going to keeping your babies safe and getting ready to welcome them.' She had read up about the risks for identical twins who shared a pla-

centa and knew how dangerous it would be
for her best friend not to follow her doctors'
advice to the letter.

She had a momentary vision of warm aqua-
marine waters, golden sands, palm trees—her
tropical holiday far, far away from the com-
mercial frenzy of Christmas in London. It had
been booked and paid for months ago and she
had been eagerly anticipating the escape. But
as she focussed on her friend's wan face, the
vision faded away. She needed to be here, and
she needed to do this for Caity. She only hoped
she'd be able to get at least a partial refund.

'Of course I'm happy to do the job for you,'
she said. She injected as much enthusiasm as
she could into her voice. And was rewarded
by the relief in her friend's eyes.

'I knew you wouldn't let me down,' Caity
said. She took a deep breath. 'I'll quickly brief
you. Longfield Manor is in Dorset, near the
coast. Very traditional. Nothing like the ultra-
contemporary Pierce Group hotels. It was owned
by my client's grandparents. But the grandfather died this year, so Oliver Pierce stepped in
to help his grandmother run it. There's a story
there but I didn't get a chance to dig into it. You
might have more luck. Christmas has always

been a big deal, and they want it even bigger and better this year.'

Marissa was determined not to let her friend see how she dreaded the thought of working on Christmas for an entire week. 'Understood,' she said.

'Everything that can be ordered has been ordered. Local staff have been briefed. You'll find all the files waiting in your inbox so you can hit the ground running. I sent them as soon as I knew you were on your way over.'

Marissa smiled. 'You were very sure I'd say yes.'

'I trusted you'd help me,' Caity said simply.

Marissa gently hugged her friend. 'You know you won't have to worry about a thing.'

'I know. I trust you implicitly. But you can get in touch with me any time.'

'I promise I'll try not to bother you.'

It had been heartbreaking when Caity had lost her first baby, and Marissa feared what state her friend might sink into if something were to go wrong with the twins. She had to step up for her. Even though immersing herself in Christmas at some staid country house hotel was the last thing she wanted to do.

At the sound of a key turning in the door,

Caity stepped back. 'Here's Tom to take me to hospital.'

Marissa greeted her friend's husband, then picked up her handbag and the shopping bag containing her solitary dinner. 'Go. The sooner you're in that hospital bed, the better.'

'Just one thing before you go. Oliver Pierce is expecting you to stay on site at Longfield Manor for the seven days before Christmas.'

'On site? For a week?'

'It's a hotel. Why would you stay elsewhere?'

Marissa would prefer to keep a distance from a client. But this was Caity's client so she really had no choice. 'Done. Can't say I like it. But done.'

'And…there's one more thing.'

A sneaky smile played around her friend's lips. Marissa knew that smile could spell trouble. 'Yes?' she said warily.

'Oliver Pierce is hot. Really hot. Movie-star hot.' She put up her hand to stop Marissa from protesting. 'I know you're on a break from dating. An overly long break in my opinion. But I respect that. I just thought you should know how gorgeous your new client is. And I believe he's single. Single, sexy and solvent.'

Marissa rolled her eyes. 'No, thank you. I won't ever get mixed up with a client again.

Totally not interested. Besides, you know I'm immune to gorgeous men. Next time—if there is ever a next time—I'll be going for ordinary, average and safe.'

Caity laughed. 'I wouldn't call Oliver Pierce safe. Not in a million years would I call him safe.'

Could this be his last Christmas at Longfield Manor? The thought troubled Oliver. If there was one thing he didn't care for, it was uncertainty. And the future of the beautiful old manor house, which had been in his family for five generations, was shrouded in uncertainty.

He stamped his feet against the cold and rubbed his gloved hands together as he observed the familiar front elevation of the house. It was lit by the soft, early-morning sun that shone from a cloudless winter sky. He never tired of admiring the building that dated back to the sixteen hundreds, its ancient walls made of the local limestone, the peaked roofs and mullioned windows, the perfection of its proportions. The surrounding gardens were stark in their winter beauty, the only splashes of colour coming from large urns overflowing with lush purple pansies, the pride and joy of his grandmother.

Oliver hadn't lived there for years, but he considered Longfield Manor his home; his grandparents, Charles and Edith, were more his parents than his parents ever had been. He had spent so much of his childhood here, an only child caught in the to-and-fro that had been his parents' disastrous marriage. And it was the refuge to which he'd fled after his mother had abandoned him when he was fifteen years old. If he honoured his late grandfather's dying wish, he would have to put Longfield Manor on the market. And there lay the uncertainty.

Just days before he took his last laboured breath at the age of eighty-seven, his grandfather had taken Oliver aside for a private, heartbreaking conversation. His grandpa had known he was dying and he'd told Oliver he feared for his beloved wife, five years his junior at eighty-two. He had shared his concern that Edith could be displaying signs of dementia. It seemed she'd had memory lapses, misplaced things, sometimes seemed confused about long-standing everyday routines, and her devoted husband was worried how she would cope after he'd gone.

It had been gut wrenching for Oliver to listen to that, but he'd owed it to the grandfather he'd adored not to show his own anguish. Grandpa had also worried that with the pending retirement of a longtime trusted manager, overseeing the running of the hotel would be too much for Edith. He'd believed the best option would be to sell, then find Edith a home, perhaps in London so she could be closer to Oliver, somewhere she could easily access the round-the-clock care she might soon need.

Oliver had been shocked, not just by the news about Granny, but also because he had never imagined Longfield Manor would be sold. He had long expected that it would pass down to him—his mother had been disinherited—and in due course to his children. Not that so far, at the age of thirty-two, he had ever met a woman who inspired thoughts of marriage and parenthood. He made very sure his girlfriends knew the score—he wasn't ready to commit.

He had immediately reassured his grandfather he would take over the hotel alongside his grandmother. Hotels were his business. He had got his love of hospitality from growing up here, absorbing what worked and what didn't from the way his grandparents ran the place. Longfield Manor was a successful and profitable business, as well as a cherished private home.

But his grandfather had asked him to think

long and hard before declaring an intention to add Longfield Manor to his portfolio. Not to make that offer out of sentimentality or obligation. Charles hadn't wanted the hotel to become a burden on his grandson. Oliver's life was in the city with his ultra-contemporary boutique hotels. And didn't he want to expand into New York? Where did a traditional hotel in the country fit into that plan? A hotel that needed hands-on management with buildings that required ongoing repair.

Oliver had acknowledged all that, and yet he fought against the idea of losing Longfield Manor. His grandfather had repeatedly asked him to agree to selling the hotel after he died. Oliver prided himself on being a hard-headed negotiator yet finally, to put Grandpa's mind at ease, he had acquiesced and said he would 'look into' selling. Now Oliver felt duty bound to honour that deathbed promise. Even if he'd had his fingers crossed behind his back at the time.

Since Grandpa's passing in August, Oliver had observed some out-of-character behaviour from his grandmother but nothing overly untoward. Many of those quirks could be, he thought, attributed to her intense grief at losing her husband of so many years. Granny was grieving, as was he, although he knew he had to keep it together for her sake. The only thing that sparked her back into her old self was discussing plans for Christmas.

His grandparents had put their hearts and souls into Christmas every year. Guests came from around the country—even the world—to share in the hotel's fabled Christmas celebrations. And Oliver was determined their first Christmas without Charles would be extra special so that his absence hopefully wouldn't be felt quite so keenly.

To that end, he had engaged an event planner with whom he had worked very successfully at his London hotels. Caity Johnston was a small, blonde dynamo who was totally on his wavelength. She had reacted to the brief on the Longfield Manor Christmas with enthusiasm, and he had been pleased she had accepted the job. However, complications with her pregnancy meant Caity had had to be hospitalised. 'Never fear,' Caity had rushed to reassure him. She had secured someone wonderful to take over from her. Marissa Gracey was the absolute best, she'd assured him.

There had been no opportunity to interview Marissa Gracey. He'd had to accept her sight unseen—and that didn't sit well with Oliver.

Marissa Gracey had become yet another uncertainty. He hoped Caity hadn't overdone the enthusiasm for her substitute. This Christmas was important. A successful celebration would not only lift his granny's spirits, it would also reassure the guests that the hotel could go on successfully without Charles. In his experience, fans of a hotel liked things to stay the same. He needed to prove to both himself and others that the future of Longfield Manor would be safe in his hands—one way or another.

But planning a traditional Christmas celebration on a grand scale was outside his area of expertise. He needed help. There were seven days to Christmas and as the celebrations went into full swing on Christmas Eve, the countdown was on. He glanced at his watch. Marissa Gracey was due to arrive in half an hour for a midmorning start. He hoped her work would be up to scratch.

Marissa swung her vintage Citroen van through the ornate iron gates that were set between high stone walls and led up to a sweeping gravel driveway lined with well-kept gardens. Even in winter the grounds of the hotel showed a certain stark grandeur. If she was here for anything other than Christmas, she'd be feeling stirrings of excitement.

Marissa had looked up the hotel's impressive website and read with interest the high-rating reviews on impartial travel sites. The reviews from guests had raved about the beauty of the buildings, the comfort of the rooms, the excellence of the food. It was clear that the hotel's guests came back again and again and one regular had described it as a 'home away from home—a very posh home, that is.'

If only she were coming here to work in summer. Or autumn. Really anytime but Christmas. The thought of the extravaganza to come made her feel queasy, but for Caity's sake she had to overcome her aversion to the job. She could do this. The back of her van was filled with bespoke Christmas ornaments from a famous London designer and all other manner of expensive and stylish decorations that would give an 'old with a new twist' feel to the festive decorations here. Apparently, the grandson of the family, Oliver Pierce, wanted to put his own stamp on the family traditions. She wondered why he would mess with a formula that clearly worked.

As the house came into view, Marissa caught her breath. It was stately and magnificent, yet not so large as to dominate the landscape. Framed by two enormous winter-bare oak trees, the hotel sat nestled into the landscape like it belonged—as it had been standing in that very spot for hundreds of years.

She thought of Oliver Pierce with a stab of… not envy—not exactly—more like curiosity, at how it must feel to be born to a place like this. To take the immense wealth that this house and the grounds that surrounded it stood for, as his due. She had grown up in a middle-class family, comfortable but not wealthy. This was a different realm altogether. And that, she had realised from reading the reviews of the hotel, was its charm. A place like this gave the guests the chance to imagine for the length of their stay that they were taking part in an exclusive house party. That was the key to Christmas at Longfield Manor, to create welcoming, intimate but extravagant festivities. A posh home away from home, where the Christmas holiday was utterly splendid and utterly without worry or stress or hours in the kitchen.

She confidently swung the van—its quirky exterior finished in a rich brown and chrome as befit its former life as a coffee van—into the circular drive that led up to the house. The discreet signage at the entrance of the hotel maintained the illusion of arriving at your own house in the country. Marissa knew there was parking around the back, but she'd been asked to check in with reception when she arrived, so she pulled the van into the closest space out front.

Once inside, she caught her breath at the splendour of the entrance hall. Ornate high ceilings, wood-panelled walls, a magnificent staircase, wooden floors laid in a centuries-old herringbone pattern, paintings in heavy gilded frames. A large arrangement of artistically styled winter-bare stems and brightly coloured berries sat in a marble urn on a tall plinth. It was all perfect, but not too perfect, which befit a house of such venerable years. She'd read that the house had been sympathetically remodelled to become a hotel, but on first glance it still retained both the grandeur and the intimacy of a private home to the privileged.

Inside, she was greeted by a charming young woman behind the reception desk. Marissa put down her small suitcase and wondered when she'd meet with the client, Oliver Pierce. She didn't have to wonder for long.

Almost immediately, the grandson of the house strode into the foyer. Suddenly, the room seemed smaller, as if he took up more space than one man should. He was taller than she'd thought he'd be, and broad shouldered in an immaculately cut dark suit. Black hair framed a handsome—a very handsome—face. Caity was right. He was hot. So hot Marissa could not help but stare. And then, when he got closer, stare some more.

'Marissa Gracey?' he said in a deep, well-spoken voice that managed to be just as attractive as his looks. 'Oliver Pierce.'

All Marissa could do was nod before he continued.

'You're right on time. That's good.'

It was as well he hadn't expected a reply because she was suddenly without a voice. She felt the colour flush hot on her cheeks then rush back to pale as a realisation struck her.

*She knew this man.*

Only he'd called himself Oliver Hughes back then. Back when they'd both been teenagers and she'd thought him the most insufferable, arrogant, rude person she had ever met. When he offered his hand for her to shake, she didn't know what to do.

# CHAPTER TWO

MARISSA'S THOUGHTS FLASHED back to when she'd been fourteen years old and deeply, desperately and very secretly in love with a sixteen-year-old boy she'd known as Oliver Hughes.

This couldn't be the same guy.

*It just couldn't be.*

Yet, he looked like him, spoke like him. Did he have a twin? If so, wouldn't they have the same surname? And why the same first name?

Oliver Hughes had been the friend of her schoolfriend Samantha's brother, Toby. Toby had been at boarding school with Oliver and brought him home to stay for a midterm break. Marissa had immediately crushed on tall, quietly spoken Oliver like only a totally inexperienced girl could. She'd jumped at any chance she could to be at Samantha's house.

But that crush had come crashing down the day she'd overheard Toby and Oliver discussing her and Samantha. Toby had asked Oliver what he thought of Sam's friend Marissa. Oliver had made a rude comment about Marissa's appearance, then both boys had sniggered in a mean, hurtful and entitled way. Marissa had been shocked, horrified and deeply hurt. It had been a first lesson painfully learned—men weren't always what they appeared to be.

Now she realised she couldn't hesitate any longer before taking Oliver Pierce's hand in a short, businesslike grasp. She'd never got even handshake-close to Oliver Hughes. It had been purely a crush from a distance. She looked up at Oliver Pierce and caught her breath. The black hair. The green eyes. His height. It had to be the same guy. Super-attractive as a teenager, devastatingly handsome as an adult. Why hadn't she researched him when she'd agreed to take on this job? She'd only looked up Longfield Manor and had trusted Caity's notes for the details of the Christmas plans.

*I'm immune to gorgeous men*, she'd boasted to her best friend.

She'd had no interest whatsoever in the hotness levels of her client.

'Welcome,' he said. 'Thank you for taking Caity's place.'

His voice was deep and resonant. More mature than at age sixteen, but somehow it sounded the same to her. Oliver Hughes had had the beginnings of a man's voice even then. *The fantasies she had had over him.* She almost gasped at the memory of the feelings he had aroused in her.

'I'm…er…glad I was able to help out, Mr Pierce,' she said.

*Not.*

As if having to fake a love of Christmas was bad enough, now she would be trapped for a week with a man she'd never forgotten. She remembered him not because of his extraordinary good looks that back then had set her teenage heart thumping, but because of how deeply he had wounded her. It had taken a long time to restore the confidence his mocking words had caused to her fragile teenage ego.

'Oliver, please,' he said.

'Sure,' she said. 'Oliver.' She felt like she was choking on his name.

He smiled. Yep, same toothpaste-commercial white teeth. Almost too perfect to be true. 'There's a lot to do,' he said. 'I'm sure Caity briefed you about how I want this year's Christmas to be better than ever?'

As he spoke, Marissa realised there was not even the merest spark of recognition in his eyes. He had no idea that they'd met before.

*If indeed they had.*

Perhaps it was an insane coincidence that this Oliver was so like teenage crush Oliver. But she didn't think so. It had to be him. But she couldn't really be sure until she investigated his surname. In the meantime, as he had not recognised her—which added further insult to his insults of sixteen years ago—she wouldn't say a thing. That would only revive the humiliation.

'Caity briefed me very thoroughly,' Marissa said, in a cool, businesslike tone, totally at odds with her inner turmoil. 'I'm looking forward to going through the timetable of events with you and meeting the local staff and suppliers Caity engaged. There are, however, questions I need to ask you, to fill in the gaps.'

'Of course. How about we set up a meeting in half an hour at my grandfather's study.' He paused and she was surprised at the flash of pain across his face. 'I mean *my* study.' He sighed. 'Grandpa died in August. I forget sometimes that he isn't here.'

'I understand,' she said, fighting the sudden empathy she felt towards this man. She knew only too well about loss in various heartbreaking ways. 'It does get better with time. Although I don't believe you ever completely get over losing someone you love.'

He looked down into her eyes—she was tall but he was taller—and she saw the pain in his eyes. 'You...?' he said.

Marissa met his gaze as she swallowed against the lump in her throat. 'My parents. Five years ago. A car accident.'

*On Christmas Eve.*

'I'm sorry.'

'I'm sorry about your grandfather.'

An awkward silence fell between them. How did that business conversation suddenly swerve to something so personal?

Oliver Pierce cleared his throat. 'Did you drive directly from London?' he said, very obviously changing the subject.

Marissa jumped at the opportunity to do so. 'Yes,' she said. 'The traffic wasn't too bad.'

Traffic was always a safe topic of conversation between strangers. It had taken three hours in her van, which wasn't as fast on the road as more modern vehicles. But she loved her van; it was different and quirky but very practical.

'I'll show you to your room.' Oliver Pierce picked up the small suitcase she had brought in with her. She had another with more clothes in the van.

'Where should I park my van?'

'If you leave the keys at the desk, someone will take your van to the garage at the back of the hotel.'

'Is it secure? There are boxes of valuable things in there.'

The moment she uttered the query she chastised herself. They were in the middle of nowhere, up a long driveway behind secure gates on a private property. Who was going to break into her van and steal Christmas decorations? She was too used to living in central London.

'Very secure,' he said. 'But I'll arrange for someone to transfer them to a storeroom, if that would make you feel better?'

'Thank you,' she said, nodding.

She followed Oliver Pierce up the magnificent carved wooden staircase. As she trailed her hand over the top of the balustrade, she thought about how many other hands must have trailed along it over hundreds of years, what stories these wood-panelled walls could tell. She also couldn't stop wondering about Oliver Pierce, possibly Hughes. How would she deal with him?

'There are ten bedrooms on this floor, all en suite, and a further ten on the next floor,' he said when they reached the first floor. 'A further twelve bedrooms are located in a converted barn. Our family lives in a separate wing.'

'It's such an amazing building,' she said, still disconcerted by the thought that this Oliver must be *that* Oliver. She felt she had to weigh up every word she said to him.

'Longfield Manor has been in my family for a long time,' he said. 'My grandparents turned it into a hotel thirty years ago.'

Oliver strode ahead of her with athletic grace. Marissa couldn't help but admire the view as she followed him. Broad shoulders, long, strong legs. He was one of those men who looked really good in a business suit.

He stopped at a door at the farther end of the corridor. 'This is your room,' he said, opening the door. 'It makes sense for you to stay here as a guest rather than stay in the village, where the rest of the staff lives or stays, and have to drive in every day.'

'Of course. I appreciate it,' she said. He would have had to pay for her to stay elsewhere so why not have her on site? It made good business sense.

But it was immediately evident that he hadn't stinted on her accommodation. Her room was spacious and elegant, with antique-style furnishing, curtains and upholstery. It had been brought into this century with a light hand that allowed its historical charm to shine through. There was nothing stuffy about the decor, no heavy dark colours or cumbersome furniture. Rather, muted colours and lush, pale carpets gave it a feel of contemporary luxury that was not at odds with the building's history. A top interior designer had obviously been employed to find the perfect balance. 'What a beautiful room,' she said, looking around her. 'Timeless and elegant.'

'My grandmother always likes to hear that kind of feedback,' he said. 'She was an interior designer when she was younger and has put her heart and soul into this place.'

'She's done a wonderful job.' Marissa paused. 'About your grandmother. It's my understanding she and your grandfather organised the Christmas festivities themselves. Will I be treading on her toes?'

'Good question,' he said.

Marissa didn't like it when people said, *good question*. It usually served to stall an answer or was a condescending response to a question they didn't think was good at all.

But Oliver Pierce spoke the words as if he meant them. 'I asked her about that before I got Caity on board. Granny said she was re-lieved that she didn't have to do all the work by herself. That even with my grandfather or-ganising it with her, the Christmas festivities were beginning to become too much.'

'That's good to hear. I know you want to make changes and I wondered how she felt about that.'

'Granny is eighty-two years young, as she likes to say. She's not resistant to change, but she'll certainly let you know what she thinks if she disagrees with anything.'

Marissa smiled, in spite of her resolve to stay distant. His words were underscored with affection and she liked that. She respected peo-ple who were close to their families—she who had been left without family and ached for their loss.

'Granny and Grandpa were partners in every sense of the word. She's struggling without him, but grateful that I can take over some of what he did. She will be sure to want to meet you as soon as possible. I'll ask her to attend our meeting.'

'I'll look forward to meeting her.' Caity had told her she'd liked Edith Pierce very much and had enjoyed working with her.

'I'll leave you to unpack. See you in half an hour.'

The second he shut the door behind him, Marissa threw her coat on the bed and reached for her phone. An internet search might help clear up the mystery of the two Olivers.

Thankfully, it was a mystery quickly solved. Oliver Pierce, according to the gossip columnists, was notoriously private. But that didn't stop stories about the handsome hotelier finding their way into the news. Oliver had changed his name from his father's name, Hughes, to his mother's name, Pierce, when he'd been about twenty-four. A bold move to make. His mother, an only child, had been a famous model and, according to well-documented gossip, it seemed her marriage to Oliver's father had been tumultuous. But to change his name? As Caity had said, there was a story there. Perhaps it was a sad one. But it was none of Marissa's business. What she'd discovered didn't make her change her mind about Oliver.

*Odious Oliver*, she'd called him in her secret thoughts for so long.

Today's Oliver seemed very personable. Charming even. She'd found herself warming to him when there was still a doubt he might not be the Oliver from her past. But now she knew the truth. She shuddered. His mean words were indelibly carved into her memory. However, that would not stop her from treating a client—Caity's client—with professional courtesy. Aside from that, she intended to avoid him as much as possible.

Marissa Gracey was gorgeous. Oliver didn't know why the fact that Caity's replacement was so attractive should come as such a shock. Perhaps because Caity had gone overboard on stressing how smart and efficient and capable her friend Marissa was. He hadn't given a thought to what the paragon might look like.

Not that the appearance of his new event planner mattered in the slightest. Of course it didn't. He never dated staff—even those on a short-term contract. An early disaster dating an assistant manager had made sure he steered clear of such ill-advised liaisons. He just wanted the event planner to have all the attributes Caity had promised that would ensure Christmas at Longfield Manor this year was outstanding.

Still, he found it disconcerting that Marissa was such a classic beauty, tall and willowy with dark hair that tumbled over her shoulders, deep blue eyes, a generous mouth, cheeks flushed pink from the cold outside. Oliver had found it hard not to stare earlier when he'd seen her waiting for him at the reception desk, elegant in narrow black trousers, high-heeled black boots and a striking purple wool coat. He'd also found himself taking surreptitious side glances at her as he showed her to her room, where she'd slipped off her coat to reveal a long-sleeved silk shirt in an abstract black-and-white pattern. While discreetly professional, the snug-fitting shirt made no secret of her curves. She really was a stunner.

She was punctual, too. He was pleased to see that Marissa arrived at his office for their meeting five minutes early. Punctuality and order were important to him, among the tools with which he'd tried to ward off the craziness of his early years. His mother had fallen pregnant with him 'accidentally' when she was at the peak of her modelling career and married his father because it was the done thing at the time. He didn't know if it had ever been a happy marriage. His earliest memories were of them arguing—noisy and angry, and worse when they'd been drinking. Every time he'd been dumped off with Granny and Grandpa, their house had been a haven of peace and unconditional love.

Had his mother loved him? She'd told him she loved him, but it was difficult for him to believe her when she'd left him so often. Every time, he'd felt abandoned. 'Mummy's working, models have to travel,' Granny used to explain as she'd wiped away his tears. His father had been in a never-quite-made-it rock band and was also away on tour a lot of the time. However, the truth was obvious to him now—a child got in the way of their complicated lives, and they took the easy route of foisting him onto others so that they didn't have to worry themselves with his care. He sometimes wondered if they had ever considered what it was like for a child to be constantly referred to— to their face—as *an accident*.

They'd shunted him into boarding school at the age of eight. His parents had then separated and reconciled several times before divorcing when he'd been thirteen. When he was fifteen, his mother had met a man who lived in New Zealand. She'd gone to visit him and hadn't come back since, except for occasional fleeting visits to England. Oliver had expected to go with her but his mother hadn't thought it appropriate for him to change schools at that stage of his studies. So she'd left him behind. Like a piece of unwanted baggage. Again.

Marissa sat down in the visitor's chair opposite from him. She put a large folder and a tablet on the desk in front of her and outlined an agenda. Professional. He liked that, too.

'Caity's already done all the hard work,' she said. 'She's organised suppliers, discussed the menus with your chefs, engaged musicians, briefed the florist, hired decorating staff and so on. As per your instruction, she's used local people wherever possible. Now it's up to me to make it happen flawlessly so your guests have the best Christmas ever.'

'Sounds like everything is on track to me,' he said.

She paused and a frown pleated her forehead. 'One thing I'm not quite sure of is the gift-giving ceremony after lunch on Christmas Day presided over by Santa Claus and Mrs Claus. I understand all the guests receive a gift from the jolly couple?'

'Oh, yes,' he said, unable to stop himself from smiling. The mention of the tradition had sparked so many happy memories from over the years. 'It's a family tradition that morphed into a hotel tradition.'

'How so?' she said, her head tilted to one side.

'When I was a child, Grandpa and Granny dressed up as Santa and his wife on Christmas morning. Apparently, they'd done that for my mother when she was a child. I loved it. When they started the hotel, it turned out the guests loved Santa and Mrs Claus, too. The hotel ceremony takes place after the long Christmas lunch.'

'I see,' she said.

Oliver wondered why a shadow passed over Marissa's face as he explained the tradition. That could mean she had happy memories of Christmas or, on the other hand, memories that were less than happy. People who spent Christmas at a hotel often included those who were escaping unhappy family situations, those with no families, people who were far away from home at Christmas, as well as the people who wanted a traditional Christmas with all the trimmings without all the work. Marissa had agreed to work Christmas Day at Longfield Manor without hesitation or demands for extra remuneration. Where would she be on Christmas Day otherwise? Or with whom?

'That sounds fun,' she said at last. 'I find it endearing that the owners of a hotel would celebrate like that with their guests. I'm wondering, though…how will it happen this year?' she said, as though carefully choosing her words.

'Without Grandpa, you mean?' he said, with a painful wrench to his gut.

She nodded.

Oliver felt overwhelmed by sadness that Grandpa wouldn't be here to play Santa. It was just another reminder that Christmas wouldn't be the same ever again. Marissa's sympathy for his loss was there in her expressive blue eyes. He looked away, unable to bear it. 'It will be me stepping into Santa's big black boots. I can do a *ho-ho-ho* with the best of them,' he said, forcing positivity into his voice.

'And your grandmother?'

'She'll be Mrs Claus as usual.' He put up his hand to stop any possible objection. 'I know I should be Grandson Claus. But the white curly hair and beard of the Santa outfit will disguise the age difference. It's all in the Christmas spirit.'

'Of course it is,' she said.

*Damn.* He suspected she could tell how upsetting he found this conversation. Oliver knew he was good at masking his feelings—he'd learned that from a very early age—so how could this woman he barely knew see through his mask?

There was a loud knock on the door, accompanied by the door opening. Granny. She never waited for a *come in* invitation before she entered the room.

He was pleased she'd chosen to join them. It must come as a shock to her every time she saw her grandson seated behind her husband's big antique desk. It was still a shock to him, too. He'd known his grandfather wouldn't live forever, but he'd wanted more years with him than what he'd been given.

He rose and came around his desk to greet her. 'Talking of my grandmother. Here she is,' he said to Marissa. She got up from her chair, too, so they stood side by side.

His grandmother swept into the room with her usual aplomb. She paused as she took in Marissa, then smiled. He hadn't seen her smile like that since Grandpa's death.

'Granny, this is Marissa Gracey. Marissa, my grandmother, Edith Pierce. Marissa is here to help us with Christmas.'

His grandmother positively beamed as she turned to Marissa. 'I know why Marissa is here. It's very good of you, my dear, to come down to us from London to help.'

'I'm glad I was able to make it,' Marissa said politely.

Granny turned back to him with a puzzled

frown. 'But Oliver darling, why did you put Marissa in Room eight?'

'It's a lovely room,' he said. 'I want her to be comfortable while she's here working with us.' Did Granny think it more appropriate for Marissa to be in the staff quarters?

'It's a very nice room,' Marissa said.

'But surely she should be in your room with you, Oliver?'

Marissa gasped. Oliver stared at his grandmother in disbelief.

'I might be old but I'm broad minded, you know. There's no need for you and your girlfriend to scurry around behind my back playing musical beds. I suggest you move her into your room right now.'

# CHAPTER THREE

Marissa stared at Edith Pierce, speechless with shock. Why would the older woman say such a thing? She glanced at Oliver, but he seemed equally shocked.

Mrs Pierce looked from her grandson to Marissa and back to Oliver again. She was an elegant older woman, beautifully groomed with silver hair cut in a short bob and discreet jewellery of the very expensive kind. A smile danced around her perfectly lipsticked mouth.

'Do I shock you? Your generation didn't invent sex, you know.'

Oliver looked mortified. He glanced at Marissa, as if beseeching her for help. But what could she do? This was his grandmother, a stranger to her.

The thought of having sex with Oliver Pierce in his bedroom sent a flush to Marissa's cheeks, those fervent teenage fantasies she'd had about him rushing back.

'I know that, Granny, but—' Oliver finally said.

Marissa found her voice. 'I'm not his—'

'Marissa is our new event planner, Granny. Remember Caity, who you liked so much, had to go into hospital to have her pregnancy monitored?'

'Of course I remember that,' Mrs Pierce said, sounding annoyed. 'My memory might fail me a little these days, but not about important things like our Christmas celebrations.'

'Marissa is her replacement. She's a very experienced event planner and comes with glowing references.'

Mrs Pierce smiled. 'You don't have to hide from me the fact she's also your girlfriend. She's lovely and—'

'She is that,' said Oliver. 'Very lovely, I mean.'

*That's not what he said about me when he was sixteen.*

'But she's not my—'

Mrs Pierce spoke over him. 'I know you like to keep your private life private, Oliver. But I'm delighted Marissa is able to spend Christmas with you, and that I get the chance to get to know her. It makes me so very happy to see you with such a beautiful girl. Smart, too, as you say.' Her words were gushing, but to Marissa they seemed sincere—if completely misguided.

The older lady paused. To gather her emotions or for dramatic effect? Marissa couldn't be sure. This was so awkward she could scarcely breathe. Oliver had to say something. It was up to him to stop this nonsense. She, Marissa, was a stranger and a contracted employee to boot. She couldn't get into an argument with the owner of Longfield Manor.

But before either of them could say anything, his grandmother continued. 'You know, Oliver, how sad I've been since my beloved Charles's death. So miserable I… I've sometimes wondered if it's worth living.' Her voice wavered as she bowed her head. Oliver looked alarmed. He stepped towards her, put a hand on her arm. Mrs Pierce looked up at her grandson. 'There seemed…nothing to look forward to.'

'Granny. You can't say that.' There was an edge of anguish to his voice.

'I just did, though, didn't I? I'm sorry. I know you're grieving him, too. But the loss of a husband is something else. Soulmates. That's a term we didn't use when we were young. But that's what we were—soulmates.'

'I know,' Oliver said. 'You were so happy with Grandpa.' It was his turn to sound bereft.

Marissa shifted from foot to foot, uncomfortable at being witness to his family's pain and loss. She was an outsider who shouldn't really be there. If she could back out of the room without them noticing her, she would.

However, the older woman seemed intent on involving her. 'But this. Marissa. I'm not jumping the gun or anything, but perhaps… Well, the prospect of seeing my grandson settled, that makes me happier than I'd imagined I'd ever be again. You know, new life and all that.'

'Granny,' said Oliver, obviously through gritted teeth. 'It's not like that. It really isn't.' He didn't look at Marissa. *Couldn't* look at her, more likely.

This was awkward. To see this tall, powerful man at a loss of what to say to this petite older woman, whom he obviously loved and respected. Did Edith Pierce really believe her to be Oliver's girlfriend? Or was it…old age speaking? She didn't know her so couldn't make a judgement. Her own grandmother had become decidedly odd in her final years.

Mrs Pierce sighed, a sound Marissa found heart wrenching. With that sigh, the older lady seemed somehow to diminish, and even her beautiful, smooth skin and expertly applied make-up couldn't hide the fact that she was frail. Marissa noticed that her cashmere cardigan hung loosely on her and that her tailored tweed skirt seemed loose at the waist.

'My first Christmas without my beloved Charles in more than sixty years. I... I don't know how I'll manage.'

Oliver put his arm around her. She was tiny, and only came up to his elbow. 'Granny, I'm here. You're not on your own.' His voice was kind and gentle.

'I know. And neither are you. You have Marissa.'

He spoke through gritted teeth. 'Granny, you really have got the wrong idea about—'

Edith Pierce aimed a sweet smile at Marissa. 'You've made an old lady very happy, my dear,' she said. 'Thank you for coming here with Oliver. He's never had a girlfriend visit Longfield Manor before, so you must be very special. I'm looking forward to getting to know you.'

Marissa had to say something in response. She cast a quick glance at Oliver but got no help from him. He seemed as stunned as she was. 'Er, me, too,' she managed to choke out. 'Getting to know you, I mean.'

Oliver Pierce had never brought a girlfriend

home before? What did that say about him? Marissa was so disconcerted she couldn't utter another word.

'Now, shall we go through our plans for Christmas?' said Mrs Pierce in a matter-of-fact tone.

Oliver shot Marissa a glance and gave the slightest shrug of his shoulders. Marissa nodded in reply.

He indicated for her and his grandmother to take seats at a round conference table in the corner of the spacious study. Feeling more ill at ease than she could ever remember, Marissa picked up her folder and tablet and followed him. Initially, she found it an effort to act normal and businesslike with the owner of Longfield Manor. Especially after Mrs Pierce had expressed so firmly her belief that she was her grandson's girlfriend. Why hadn't Oliver denied it more vehemently?

But once seated at the table, Oliver's grandmother became pure businesswoman, alert and savvy when it came to finalising the plans for the hotel's Christmas. She was totally on top of things, including the financials. She referred to her meetings with Caity and expressed her pleasure at the way the traditional Christmas celebrations were to be enlivened with some more contemporary twists. She also liked the idea of the new designer ornaments and decorations. And was in full agreement with the innovative vegetarian and vegan additions to the menu, as more guests were requesting those alternatives to the traditional fare.

'Well done, Marissa,' she said, as she viewed the final presentation on Marissa's tablet. She seemed very much the competent, well-established owner of the hotel. Perhaps the girlfriend confusion had been an aberration.

'I'm glad you approve,' Marissa said, feeling as though she'd passed an exam.

Edith—she'd asked Marissa to call her by her first name—turned to Oliver. 'Where did you say you first met Marissa?' she asked.

'I didn't say,' he said. He looked to Marissa and back again to his grandmother. 'But…it was through a mutual friend.'

Caity. That was what he believed and it was true. Their mutual friend Caity had indeed organised their meeting for Marissa to take over from her while she was in hospital. But it was also true in another context, given he'd actually first met her through his friend Toby, brother to her friend Samantha, when they were teenagers. Oliver appeared to have no memory of that first meeting all those years ago, but she wasn't about to remind him of it. Did he still see Toby? She and Toby's sister had lost touch after Samantha had moved to a different school.

'The best way to meet your life partner,' his grandmother said approvingly. 'I don't like the idea of these dating apps.'

Oliver spluttered an indecipherable reply.

*Life partner?*

Marissa was so astounded she had to stop her mouth from gaping open. Yet, secretly, she found it amusing to see this hot, super-successful tycoon, who had been so vile to her years ago, shocked speechless by his grandmother. How the tables had turned.

Despite that, she was beyond relieved when the meeting concluded and Edith left the room. She waited with Oliver, near the door, until she could be sure the older woman had definitely gone and wouldn't overhear her. She swung around to face Oliver. 'What was that about? Why did you allow your grandmother to believe I was your girlfriend?' She wasn't speaking as contractor to client; his grandmother's absurd assumptions had swung them beyond that.

'I did not. I explained who you were.' He appeared very sure of himself, yet she could tell he was shaken by the encounter with his grandmother.

'You didn't outright deny it. And I didn't know her well enough to contradict her. Although I did try. You noticed I did try. It was so awkward for me.'

He gestured with his hands. 'I'm sorry, Marissa. Granny took me by surprise. You are here to do a job, we have no personal connection and it was…unprofessional of me not to try harder to stop her. I can only say in my defence that I was stunned almost speechless.'

Marissa had been just about to accuse him of being unprofessional, so that somehow took the wind out of her sails. What family drama had she found herself caught up in here?

'I was so embarrassed. Where on earth did your grandmother get the idea I was your girlfriend? What did you tell her about me that would have made her think that?'

Oliver shrugged broad shoulders. He had discarded his suit jacket during the course of their meeting and his tailored linen shirt did nothing to hide the ripple of muscle beneath. Gone was the gangly teenager she remembered. Oliver Pierce was built.

*But she was immune to gorgeous guys.*
Wasn't she?

'Nothing. I told her you were replacing Caity to work with us on Christmas.'

'That's all?'

'That's all,' he said emphatically. 'She's very old and has recently had some memory issues, but nothing like this level of confusion.'

Marissa took a moment to answer. 'I see.' She took another moment. 'I can tell you care very much for your grandmother,' she said carefully.

'I do. She was more a mother to me than my own mother, her daughter.'

Really? She would love to ask for more details. But the way his face closed up and his green eyes shadowed, stopped her from asking. It was none of her business.

But his grandmother mistaking her for her grandson's *life partner*-status girlfriend was very much her business. She realised he felt uncomfortable about the situation. But not as uncomfortable as she did. She had to work here for the next week.

'Can you please clear up the misunderstanding with her as soon as you can?' she said. 'I'll feel awkward dealing with her until you do.'

'I understand that. Thank you for your patience and kindness towards her,' he said. He took a deep breath and paced the space in front of his desk before coming to a halt to face her. 'But here's the thing. I haven't seen Granny smile like that since before Grandpa got ill.'

'What do you mean?'

'The way she smiled at you. The look on her face when she said how happy the thought of us—' he cleared his throat '—uh, of us being together, how happy that made her feel.'

'But she got it wrong, didn't she?'

'Very wrong.' He looked down at her, his eyes narrowed, his expression intent. 'But what if she got it right?'

Marissa took a step back from him. 'What are you saying?'

'Would it be asking too much for you to pretend to be my girlfriend for the week you are here?'

*'What?'* She was too stupefied to say anything more.

'I want you to pretend to be my girlfriend to make my grandmother happy and give her a wonderful Christmas—her first since she lost my grandfather.'

She shook her head in disbelief. 'You can't be serious.' She realised she had crossed her arms over her chest, and she had to force herself to uncross them.

'I know it's out there, but you can see how

frail she is, and how unhappy. She really took to you, although I have no idea why she thinks you're my girlfriend.'

'My own grandmother got a bit, well, eccentric is the kind way to put it, when she got older. Is Edith...?' This conversation was getting surreal.

'Before he died, my grandfather told me he was worried Granny might be displaying signs of dementia. You know, memory loss, forgetting things. I haven't seen serious signs of it myself, apart from some minor lapses that I could put down to the loss of her husband, and possible fears about her future. But this. This has shocked me and, to tell the truth, the extent of her delusion frightened me.'

Marissa frowned. 'She seemed very *compos mentis* to me when we were going over the Christmas plans.'

'She did. As sharp as she's always been. Which makes this girlfriend thing hard to understand. Unless it is a sign of...of mental deterioration.'

'Or wishful thinking, perhaps?'

'What do you mean?' he said.

'Your granny seemed so happy about the idea of us being a couple. Perhaps she's become aware of her own mortality and wants her grandson to be settled. You know, ready to produce the next generation of your family. The walls of the downstairs corridor are lined with portraits of your ancestors. There are more in here.' She indicated the panelled walls, the bronze bust of some revered past Pierce on the bookshelf. 'She might be clutching at straws. Are you the oldest son?'

She couldn't meet him in the eye, especially as the fantasies she'd had about them being a couple when they were teenagers flashed again through her mind. Although her brain might dismiss those feelings, her body knew only too well that the attraction still simmered, no matter how deeply she tried to stomp on it. Pretending to be the girlfriend of this excitingly handsome man would be madness.

'I'm an only child,' he said. 'And the only grandchild, in fact.'

'There you have it.'

'You could be right,' he said slowly. 'Although I thought Granny had long given up trying to matchmake me with her friends' granddaughters.'

'Perhaps she's muddled me up with one of them.'

'I doubt it. None of them are as beautiful as

you are,' he said dismissively. Had he really said that so casually?

'Oh,' she said, unable to meet his eye. He certainly hadn't found her beautiful when he'd first met her. Still, it was hard not to feel flattered.

He paused, tugged at the collar of his shirt. 'I know this is an off-the-wall plan. Not something I could ever have imagined I would propose. But I'm worried about Granny, and it seems nothing could make her happier than the belief that you and I are together.'

Marissa was still reeling at the thought of it. 'I suppose there's the chance that she might have forgotten about this girlfriend notion already?'

'Unlikely, with you around to remind her of it.'

'I could leave. It would be difficult to find you another event planner at this stage but I—'

'No,' he said with a dismissive gesture. 'You going could make her worse.'

'Or we could continue to deny it. Any relationship, I mean.'

'It would be more unsettling for her if we have to continuously deny it. Pretend to be together and we can all get on with the job of making this a memorable Christmas.'

She frowned. 'You're serious about this?'

'I am.'

'I… I don't know what to say.'

'*Yes* would be a start.' A hint of a smile lurked around the grim set of his mouth.

Slowly, she shook her head. 'I really don't know that this would be a good idea.'

'Name your price.'

'Excuse me? I'm not for sale!' He seemed different. But it appeared he hadn't changed at all since he was sixteen. He was still arrogant and overbearing. No. He was worse.

'Aargh,' he said, pushing his fingers through his hair. 'That came out wrong. Of course I don't think you're for sale. I meant we could make the pretence an extension of your role as our event planner. Pretend to be my girl-friend and I could add a substantial bonus to your fee.'

'Not interested,' she said, shaking her head. Exchanging personal services for money? Not happening. Never happening. And she had vowed never, ever again to get involved with a client. That was how she'd met the Christmas mistletoe disaster boyfriend.

'In fact, I think I should leave,' she said. 'Now. Your grandmother has a good handle on what to do for Christmas, as our meeting showed, and that will solve the girlfriend problem.'

'I fear it wouldn't.' He looked up to the ornately patterned ceiling and back to her. His black hair stuck up in ruffles, which had the effect of making him look more vulnerable. Vulnerable? Oliver Pierce? *Huh*.

She frowned. 'Why is that?'

'I'm worried how she might react to you leaving so abruptly. What if she blamed herself? I couldn't bear it if she reacted badly.' He looked somewhere over her shoulder, not meeting her eyes. 'It's difficult for me to talk about personal stuff. Especially to a stranger. But given you've suffered your own loss, you might understand.' He swallowed hard. 'Granny is all I've got. She and Grandpa pretty much raised me. My parents… Well, they weren't that interested in their son.'

Marissa thought about the gossip pages she'd read. The supermodel mother. The rock-musician father. The way Oliver had felt the need to change his surname. His upbringing had been so different from her happy, secure childhood.

'Your parents. Where are they now?'

'My mother lives in New Zealand. I haven't seen her for years. My father took off a long time ago. He has another family now, some-where in Cornwall.'

'I'm sorry,' she said. They felt like such inadequate words in the face of his loss, but she couldn't think of anything better to say.

'Don't be,' he said with a bitter twist to his mouth. 'They're no great loss. It's my grand-parents who suffered when their daughter left. And now that Grandpa is gone—'

'You're all she has,' she said softly. 'In terms of family, I mean.'

He nodded. 'She's eighty-two and I want to hold on to her for as long as I can. I want to keep her happy. I want to do whatever I can to help her stave off possible dementia. And if that means pretending a woman I've only just met is my girlfriend—how did she put it?'

'Your *life-partner* girlfriend.'

'Yes. That. If I have to pretend to be in a re-lationship that doesn't exist with a beautiful stranger to make Granny happy for her first Christmas without Grandpa, then I will. If that stranger is willing.'

Not quite a stranger, but he didn't know that. Should she tell him? What would be the point? Their first meeting was so long ago, it wasn't surprising that he didn't remember her. She didn't remember other boys she'd met at that time. Only Oliver had lodged himself in her memory.

'I'm here for seven days,' she said. 'What would happen after that?'

He shrugged. 'I'd tell her we'd broken up. That wouldn't surprise her. I don't have long relationships.' His mouth twisted. 'Much as Granny would like to see me married, I'm not interested in being tied down.'

Why did that not surprise her? He had ranked high in a gossip page's list of elusive, eligible bachelors.

But he'd made her think. She empathised only too well with his fierce love for his grandmother. She'd lost her parents she'd adored in the accident. The only grandmother she'd known, her mother's mother, had died of a stroke just weeks afterwards brought on, the doctors said, by shock. Of her immediate family, her brother Kevin was all she had left. But Kevin hadn't been able to bear the thought of a Christmas without his mother and father and had escaped to Australia for the Christmas after the accident. He'd met a wonderful girl while in Sydney and had settled there. He and his lovely wife, Danni, meant everything to her but distance made things difficult.

She turned away from him, took a few paces

forward and then turned back. 'If—and I said *if*—I were to agree to be your pretend girl-friend, how would it work?'

'I don't know. We'd have to work it out to-gether. Figure out something you were com-fortable with, but that seemed genuine. Does that seem reasonable to you?'

Oliver waited for her reply. He was so tall, so powerful, so very handsome, but she sensed again that surprising vulnerability. Awareness of him as a man shot through her like a siz-zling electric current. He had been a teenage crush, but her attraction had been intense and no less real because of her age. Although long dormant, it might not take much to revive that attraction. She might want to be of help, that was her nature, but her own emotional safety needed to be considered, too.

*Be careful, Marissa.*

'I suppose so,' she said slowly. 'It's a lot to take on.'

'Understood,' he said.

But she saw hope flicker in his eyes and it chipped away at her resolve to walk away and drive her van back to London. He'd shown her a different side to him, one she hadn't imagined he possessed. He loved his grand-mother, and she would be doing a good turn for a woman who had lost not only her soul-mate husband but also, it seemed, her daughter. And acting as this man's pretend girlfriend could be, she had to admit, a fun distraction at a time of year she found distinctly depressing.

Fun, yes, but dangerous too, her common sense warned her. It was dangerous that she found this man just as hot as she had when she'd been a teenager. But she was thirty years old now, and no stranger to heartbreak and disillusion when it came to men. As long as she stayed aware of that danger, kept her guard up, there should be no risk to her emotions.

'Reasonable would not mean sharing your bedroom,' she said firmly. 'Let's get that straight up front.'

'Of course not. I'd tell Granny we...uh... weren't ready to be that public about our relationship.' The lie slipped out so easily it gave her a shiver of concern.

'And there would be no payment, no bonus, required,' she added. 'It would be purely an act of compassion on my part to help a lonely, bereaved old lady over the Christmas period.' That would ensure she kept the upper hand. She would be doing him a favour rather than being beholden to him.

'If that's the way you want it.'

She sighed. 'I have to say up front that I don't like lies and dishonesty—and the fake-girlfriend thing would be one big fat lie.'

His face tightened. 'I don't like lies, either. If there's one way to get on my wrong side, it's to lie to me. But for Granny's sake, I'd think of it as a kind of charade.'

'An extension of the Christmas celebration?'

'Something like that, I guess.' He raked his fingers through his hair again. 'Hell, Marissa. I've never done anything like this before. I don't know how it might work. But when I saw how happy she was at the idea of us together...'

He seemed so genuine. So committed. She wanted to help. 'I'll do it,' Marissa said. 'I'll pretend to be your girlfriend for seven days.'

# CHAPTER FOUR

OLIVER LOOKED DOWN at Marissa, searching her lovely face. Had she really accepted his proposition without requiring financial recompense? Or any other reward? Purely from the goodness of her heart?

For his grandmother's sake he wanted to believe that. Needed to believe that. Yet, his parents' treatment of him had made him cynical and distrustful, even as a child. Had he made a huge mistake in trusting this stranger with his off-the-wall idea? What was in it for her?

His life in London as a successful hotelier had only deepened that early cynicism. In business, but also when it came to dating. He'd become used to dealing with women with ulterior motives. For some people, money seemed to be the most attractive thing about another person. The wealthier he'd got, the more appealing he—or his bank balance—seemed to become to women.

But he wasn't looking for long-term relationships—a short-term affair with a negotiated use-by date was more his style. An affair where both partners knew the score, and nobody got hurt. Pleasure, fun and a pain-free goodbye. Not that he had a rotating list of lovers—in fact, he lived a large part of his life alone and celibate. Relationships were difficult. Love was a goal that had always remained out of his reach.

There'd been one woman who had tempted him to break his self-imposed rules on commitment. Sonya was a journalist, covering the opening of the Pierce Haymarket. She'd been vibrant, clever, gorgeous. He'd been enthralled by her, let himself dream of a future with her. Then had been shocked to the core when she'd told him she was polyamorous, he was one of several lovers and that was how she wanted it to stay. Oliver had respected her life choice—but he'd wanted a one-on-one exclusive relationship. The breakup had left him lonely, miserable and plagued by feelings he hadn't been enough for her. As he hadn't been enough for his parents to want to keep him.

Marissa looked up at him, a challenge in her clear blue eyes, a slight smile curving her lips. For a moment he felt mesmerised by that unexpected smile, and the way it brought into play a very cute dimple in her right cheek. 'Now that I've accepted, please don't tell me you're having second thoughts?' she said. 'Because I'm looking forward to starting the charade.'

How did she guess the doubt that had slithered its way into his certainty?

'Of course I haven't changed my mind,' he said firmly, to convince himself as well as her. 'Making sure my grandmother enjoys this first Christmas without Grandpa is important to me. I appreciate you agreeing to help. I can't thank you enough.' He couldn't say to anyone that it might be the last Christmas at Longfield Manor if selling became the most realistic option.

'So we're really going to do this?' she said.

'Yes,' he said. 'Yes, and yes.'

On reflection, he couldn't see why she would have an ulterior motive, or where it could lead. Caity had stressed her friend's honesty and integrity. Perhaps Marissa was exactly what she seemed to be—a kind person who had let herself get talked into his scheme because it would make an old woman happy for the holidays. 'And the timing is good,' he said.

'Why so?' she asked, again with that appealing tilt of her head.

'You're not known to anyone here and I'll

need to introduce you to the hotel staff anyway as the person who is here to help us with
Christmas.'

'And at the same time, you can introduce
me as your girlfriend?'

'Who happens to be a professional event
planner.'

'Who also knows Caity, and so it seemed
logical I would come to help you.'

'On both a personal and professional basis.'

She raised her dark eyebrows on the word
*personal* and he wondered if she was waver-
ing. But she nodded.

'And if anyone asks why you hired Caity
instead of me in the first place?' she queried.

'I'll say we didn't want to mix business and
pleasure but with Caity out of commission it
seemed only natural for you to step in, as you
were going to be coming here to celebrate
Christmas with me anyway,' he offered.

'That makes a lot of sense,' she said approvingly. 'Straight away, we need to formulate a
strategy and get it clear in our heads.' Caity
had said her friend was formidably efficient.
Why would she be any different when formu-
lating a plan for a mock-relationship?

'Understood,' he said. 'But we'll have to create that strategy on the fly. There are no rules to follow. No precedent to guide us.'

'If there are, I don't know of them. I guess The Complete Book of Faking a Relationship doesn't exist.'

She laughed, a warm, delightful laugh at their complicity. For a flash of a moment he thought the way she laughed sounded familiar. But that couldn't be. He met so many people in the hospitality business, and he had no specific memory of ever having met her. Perhaps she'd momentarily reminded him of some passing acquaintance.

'That book certainly isn't in our library here,' he said, taking his turn to laugh, a laugh that felt a little rusty. There hadn't been much opportunity for jollity since his grandfather's death. Besides, he wasn't known as a jovial, laugh-out-loud kind of guy. 'Serious with a tendency to brood,' was how his old friend Toby often described him. Oliver didn't mind the serious label, but that didn't mean he was humourless.

'Strategy one, we don't tell any other person about what we're doing,' he said. 'Not even Caity.'

Marissa nodded. 'I was about to suggest the very same thing. Safer that way.'

'We don't want leaks.'

'We also need to get our stories straight about how we met. It could be disastrous if we contradicted each other.'

'True. Shall we say we met at an event at the Pierce Soho hotel that Caity had organised?' he said.

'Inspired idea,' she said. 'When did we meet? Why not first week of November?'

'We're a relatively new couple?' he said. That would be believable. He wasn't known for lengthy relationships.

'Yes, that could be a good cover if we make any errors in our knowledge of each other.'

'Quick quiz,' he said. He tried to think of the things people got to know about each other in the first weeks of a new relationship. 'Your birthday?'

'Twenty-seventh of February. Yours?'

'August twentieth.'

'Favourite food?'

'Chocolate,' she said with a wicked grin. 'Okay, maybe not. I'll go for Italian.'

'You?'

'I'll go with Italian, too.'

She laughed. 'One thing at least we have in common.'

'Where did you grow up?' he asked.

'Putney, mostly. You?'

'Between London and Dorset. Whatever best suited my parents' peripatetic lifestyle. My grandparents used to have a London townhouse until they had to sell it.'

'Oh?' she said, the one word a question.

He turned to look at a painting of Longfield's famous walled garden that his grandfather had commissioned not long before he passed. 'They were very wealthy until they lost most of their money in an unwise investment of a big insurance company. That's why they turned Longfield Manor into a hotel.'

'I didn't know that.'

'But you would be expected to if you were my girlfriend.'

'Agreed,' she said, but he could see she was shocked. 'How awful for them.'

'Grandpa and Granny are canny with money. They managed to claw back much of their fortune.'

'Good to know,' she said. He wouldn't mention that his grandparents had been early investors in The Pierce Group and had done very well out of that investment.

'Where do you live now?' she said.

'In the penthouse apartment at the top of Pierce Soho.'

'Nice,' she said. 'I live in a mansion block apartment in West Kensington.'

'A good part of London. That must be very nice, too,' he said.

'I inherited it from my godmother,' she said. 'She was my mother's best friend.' He could hear the sadness that tinged her voice. If she'd inherited, that meant her godmother must have passed. Another loss.

'I'm sorry,' he said. 'For the loss of your god-mother.'

'She was very special,' was all she said. She paused. 'Back to the get fake agenda.'

He laughed again. 'That's one way of putting it,' he said.

'We have to take it seriously, but not too seriously. If you know what I mean.'

'I think I do,' he said slowly. 'Otherwise, the relationship might not seem believable. Granny is quite astute. When she's not inventing girl-friends for me, that is.'

'I can see that,' Marissa said with another smile. 'With that in mind, we should try to be discreet. A private couple. No exaggerated public displays of affection, for example, to try and signal we're together. I'm not that kind of person and I suspect—judging by the very short time we've known each other—you're not, either.'

'Quite right,' he said, again amazed at her perception.

He did not like his private life exposed to the world. His very beautiful mother had been a magnet for the press and unfortunately, it had not been uncommon for drunken incidents outside nightclubs to be splashed across the tabloid newspapers. Too often, there had been a finger-wagging mention that she was the mother of a young son. His father, as handsome as his mother was beautiful, had got off more lightly. It seemed to be an expectation that a rock musician would be hedonistic, a suspected consumer of illegal drugs, a bad father.

'That said, to be convincing, there will have to be some outward signs of a supposed inner… uh…passion,' she said, not meeting his gaze. She flushed high on her cheekbones, which served to make her blue eyes even bluer and emphasise the creaminess of her skin. 'But again, not too exaggerated.'

Passion. Marissa. He had to force his mind away from such arousing thoughts.

*She was out of bounds.*

He cleared his throat. 'What would be on the

list of approved hinting-at-passion behaviour? Holding hands?'

She nodded. 'Definitely. But not while we're in a business situation. If we were really boyfriend and girlfriend, we wouldn't be flaunting our relationship in front of the staff. Especially when I'm working for the hotel on behalf of Caity.'

'Flaunting only allowed in front of my grandmother.'

'Quite right. But again, a discreet flaunting. Nothing that would embarrass her.'

'After what Granny has said today, I doubt that we could embarrass her. It might be more the other way around.'

Marissa laughed again. Her laughter seemed to lighten the atmosphere of this traditional room, to invite mischief into a place that might never have witnessed it.

'I know exactly what you mean,' she said. 'I really didn't know what to say or where to look when she told us that our generation didn't invent sex.'

'Me, too. All the while fighting off any images from entering my brain of my ancient grandparents indulging in what we didn't invent.'

'Please,' she said, her eyes dancing. 'I'm going to try and forget you ever said that.'

He found himself laughing, too. 'So we're agreed, just enough flaunting to make us seem believable.'

'Yes. Perhaps a discreet brushing of a hand across an arm. A low-voiced exchange of what could be perceived to be private talk between lovers. Enough to make it believable.'

She paused, looking thoughtful. 'Actually, I think that might be the secret of making this work. We try to behave as though we really are in a relationship. When we're not sure what's appropriate behaviour, we conjure up thoughts of what we would do if we really were together and act on that.'

He looked down at her. Her dark hair was pulled back in a high ponytail, which drew attention to the perfect oval of her face. Her eyes were the deep, rich blue of the delphiniums his grandfather had so prized in his spring garden. He could not keep his eyes from her lush mouth with its Cupid's bow top lip, defined with glossy pink lipstick.

He cleared his throat. 'What would we do if I—behaving as though us being a couple were real—felt the urge to kiss you?'

*'What?'*

'If we were in a relationship, I would want to kiss you.'

He wanted to kiss her now. And the urge had nothing to do with pretending. She was so beautiful, and every minute he spent with her his attraction to her grew. Had it only been a few hours? Lust at first sight? But he couldn't let himself think this way, couldn't let her know how appealing he found her. The end-game was to help Granny. And finish the charade after seven days. 'And you might want to kiss me. If we were for real, I mean.'

Her dark eyelashes fluttered and she looked away from him and back. 'I…er… I guess. A light, affectionate kiss in front of others when appropriate would be on the cards.'

'We probably wouldn't want our first kiss in front of others to look like our first kiss ever. That might give the game away.'

'What do you mean?'

'I mean a practice kiss might be in order.'

Her eyes widened. 'Here? Now?'

'Now is as good a time as any.' He glanced down at his watch. 'Time is marching on. I need to introduce you to the staff. They'll soon be arriving to help decorate the Christmas trees and whatever else you want them to do.'

'The five fully decorated Christmas trees,

each of which would normally take me an entire day to complete and which we need to get up ASAP? I'll try not to panic at the prospect of that.' She nodded thoughtfully as if kissing him was something to be checked off the list of pretend intimacies. 'Seriously. Yes. If we need to practise a kiss, now might be the time to do it.'

She took a step closer. Her eyes were wide with more than a hint of nervousness—a feeling he reciprocated. She bit her lower lip with her top teeth, which drew his eyes again to her mouth—so eminently kissable. She lifted her chin to bring her face closer to his. An atmosphere that had been amicable and warmed by laughter suddenly seemed fraught with tension. Her shoulders hunched up around her neck. She didn't seem to want him to kiss her. He wouldn't touch her without consent. He froze. What had he started?

Then she laughed, her delightful laugh that seemed already familiar. 'This is seriously weird, isn't it? Both of us holding back. I've been kissed before and I'm sure as heck you have been, too. If we need to practise, let's go for it.'

Before he could formulate his strategy for the kiss, she kissed him. She put her hands on his shoulders and planted a kiss on his mouth. Her mouth was firm and warm and fit his as if it was meant to be. But before he could relax into the kiss, it was over. She laughed again, but this time her laughter was high-pitched and tremulous. She flushed high on her cheeks. 'So, ice broken, we've kissed. Okay?'

'That's not much of a kiss,' he said, his voice husky. 'I think we could do better.'

Her eyes widened and her mouth parted. 'Er, okay,' she murmured.

He dipped his head to kiss her gently at first then, questing, exploring, her kiss in return tentative. When she responded, he deepened the kiss. She gave a little moan, which sent his arousal levels soaring. When she wound her arms around his neck to bring him closer, his arms circled her waist to pull her tighter. '*This* is a kiss,' she murmured against his mouth before returning to the kiss with increasing enthusiasm.

For practise purposes that was probably as far as they needed to go. But she felt so good in his arms. He didn't want to stop. Her scent was intoxicating, roses and vanilla and something indefinably hers. He traced the seam of her lips with the tip of his tongue, and she responded with her tongue. The kiss deepened into something hungry and passionate and totally unexpected. He wanted this kiss to be for real.

*He wanted more than this kiss.*

He scarcely registered the knock on the door when it came. He just wanted to keep on kissing Marissa. Then there was another knock. And his grandmother's familiar voice. 'Oliver, I wanted to ask—'

Marissa sprung back from his embrace. He caught a glimpse of flushed cheeks, her mouth swollen from his kisses, a flash of panic in her eyes, before he turned to face his grandmother.

'Granny,' he managed to choke out from a constricted voice. He tried not to make it obvious that his breath was coming in short gasps. He probably had Marissa's lipstick on his face and he swiped his mouth with the back of his hand.

'Edith,' Marissa said, smoothing down her top where it had come untucked from her trousers, pushing back her hair from her face. He noticed her hands weren't steady.

'You two,' said Granny with a fond smile, as she looked from him to Marissa and back again. 'I don't know why you tried to hide it from me. I knew you were together the second I saw you. And I couldn't be happier about it.'

Their first test. And they'd passed.

'We realised it was pointless to deny our relationship any longer,' Oliver said. 'Especially when you're so perceptive.'

His grandmother beamed in response. The plan was already working if she could look that happy from simply observing their kiss. Still, he found it difficult to look at Marissa—so delightfully sensuous in his arms just seconds before. Could she tell that kiss had been suddenly, urgently *real*?

'We're happy to have your blessing,' said Marissa.

Was she overdoing it? *Blessing?* But it seemed she knew exactly the right thing to say.

'You have my blessing indeed,' Granny said with another big smile. 'I'm looking forward to being a grandmother-in-law.'

Marissa was unable to stifle her shocked gasp.

But Oliver knew they had a plan, and he was going to work within the constraints. He wasn't exactly sure whether his grandmother was serious or teasing them.

'Granny, that's going too far. Marissa and I only started dating last month. Our relationship is still new. I don't want you to scare her off by getting ahead of yourself.'

Granny looked contrite. Again, he wasn't sure if she was playing them. 'Of course, darling. I won't say a word about marriage or even great-grandchildren.' Oliver protested but she put up her hand to stop him. 'I'll leave you two alone.'

'Wasn't there something you wanted to ask me?' Oliver said.

Granny gave a dismissive wave of her hand and a smug smile. 'That can wait,' she said as she closed the study door behind her.

Oliver turned to Marissa. She was shaking with the effort of suppressing a fit of the giggles. 'Flaunting it to Granny went well,' she choked out. 'Maybe too well.'

Oliver groaned and put his hand to his forehead. 'Sorry about the great-grandchildren thing.'

'I hope I hid my shock.'

'You hid it well, better than I did. In fact, you performed perfectly. Especially when we were caught by surprise. Thank you.'

'Edith's reaction proved we're believable in our roles,' she said. 'It's a good start.'

That kiss had been only too believable—and only too enjoyable. He had not intended for the kiss to go that far. He couldn't let it happen again. That surge of passion had been a lapse of judgement.

*But she had seemed to enjoy the kiss as much as he did.*

And that would make it difficult for him to hold back on kissing her again.

# CHAPTER FIVE

*WHAT HAD SHE DONE?*

Marissa turned away from Oliver, desperately trying to conceal how shaken she'd been by his kiss. Not a practice kiss. Not a pretend kiss. A passionate kiss that teased and aroused. She had responded as if she hadn't been kissed for a year. Which, in truth, she hadn't. But it had been more than banked-up carnal hunger. Not just any kiss but a kiss with *him*. She was reeling with the realisation of how much she'd liked it, how his kiss had made her dizzy with desire.

*How she wanted more kisses.*

If the kiss had been with anyone else but Oliver Pierce, who knows where she might have wanted to take it?

That wasn't how it was meant to be. This game of pretend couldn't work if real feelings and real desires entered into it. That could lead to disaster.

She made a further fuss of tidying her hair. Then turned back to pick up her folder and tablet. 'The practice kiss served its purpose. But I don't think we need to…to go that far again.'

'You're right,' he said, his voice gruff.

'We know we can be convincing and that's all that was required.'

'Yes,' he said. He was looking somewhere over his shoulder. Did he feel, like she did, that the kiss had got out of hand? She didn't know him well enough to ask.

'We're agreed on that, then?'

He nodded.

She looked down at her watch, staged a gasp of surprise. 'Look at the time. There's so much to do today.'

He looked back at her. To her relief, his glance said *business as usual*. 'First step, introduce you to the staff, as we agreed.'

'Then I'll need to get my van unloaded and be directed to the storeroom where all the rest of the Christmas decorations are kept.'

'Granny can help with that,' he said.

'About that.' She looked directly up at him. 'Oliver, I can't do my best work if Edith is interrogating me about our *relationship*. Would you mind if I politely say to her that it's all still too new and…er…precious for me to be discussing it? Pretty much what you said to her just then?'

'I'll back you up by saying the same thing when she inevitably starts to grill me.'

'Good. That's what we'd do if it was a real relationship.'

He frowned. 'There's something I didn't think to ask you. Is there a *real relationship* waiting for you back in London?'

'No. I broke up with someone about this time last year.'

She'd caught awful Aaron kissing his work colleague under the mistletoe at his company Christmas party—a serious kiss that made her instantly aware he must be sleeping with her. He hadn't even tried to deny it, and the woman concerned had sent her a glance of gloating triumph. It had been a sickening, heartbreaking moment as she had really liked Aaron and thought they were exclusive.

'There hasn't been anyone serious since. To be honest, I haven't wanted there to be. What about you?' she said.

'No one serious. I can't afford to let anything get in the way of growing my business. A new London hotel is in the planning stage. That's confidential, of course.'

She noted he said *anything* not *anyone*, which was telling.

'So, no one is going to come barging down here to Dorset to protest if anything slips out about us. As a *couple* I mean.'

'Not from my side. No.'

'Okay, then, it seems like two resolutely single people have found each other,' she said, forcing a light-hearted tone. 'Or that's our story, anyway.'

'You're good at improvising,' he said. 'Very good.'

'A lot of marketing is about selling a story, so I suppose you could say that. What I have to be careful of is that I don't overembellish our story. I have a tendency to do that.'

He smiled. 'Just stick to the facts, ma'am.'

She smiled back. 'You mean our made-up facts?'

'If in doubt, leave it out.'

'A suggestion that I'll try to stick to.' She paused. 'Nothing like a cliché or two to sort things out.'

He laughed. 'Clichés developed for a reason. They might be overused but we know exactly what they mean.'

Oliver was transformed when he laughed; his green eyes, warmed, the somewhat grim set of his mouth curved upwards, even his rigid posture seemed to relax. Caity had been right. He was hot. And he had never looked hotter than at this moment.

And her reaction to that kiss warned her not to give in to the attraction that time had not dimmed.

Even more of a problem was that, contrary to anything she could have imagined, she was beginning to like him. And that was seriously disconcerting, considering for how long she had nurtured her dislike.

Oliver introduced her to the hotel manager, Cecil Bates, a grey-haired man whom Oliver told her was on the point of retirement. He seemed warm and kind, but she could also see him being tough when necessary, and she began to see why this hotel had such a five-star reputation for comfort and good service.

'Cecil truly was Grandpa's right-hand man and will be sorely missed. Granny doesn't know that he's handed in his resignation,' Oliver explained in an undertone, after they'd left Cecil's office. 'Grandpa's death and the changes that brought with it are enough for her to deal with right now.'

She frowned. 'Edith will have to know soon, though, won't she? It seems a bit unfair to keep her in the shadows simply because she's elderly.'

He shook his head. 'It's not that at all. There might be other changes happening next year. I just want her to enjoy her Christmas without unnecessary worry.'

Marissa shrugged. She had the distinct impression Edith might not appreciate being kept out of the loop. Was Oliver being thoughtful or controlling? But it was none of her business. Nor were those mysteriously hinted at *changes*. On Christmas Day she'd be out of here and heading back to London, free of Christmas and Oliver Pierce and his family. In the meantime, she had to make sure everything between her and Oliver stayed on an even keel.

*No more passionate kissing.*

And certainly no more thinking about how exciting and arousing that kissing had been.

She immediately liked the assistant manager, Priya Singh. Priya was the lovely woman who had greeted her when she'd arrived at the hotel. Priya seemed around her age, and Marissa straight away knew she would enjoy working with her. Priya's smile was warm when Oliver introduced her as his girlfriend and explained she was stepping in for Caity.

'I liked Caity so much. Fingers crossed all

goes well for her. If you need help with any-thing, just let me know,' she said to Marissa. 'Christmas at Longfield Manor is so special. The extra work involved is worth it to make it the best ever Christmas this year.'

Oliver thanked Priya before he steered Marissa away. 'Granny just texted me. She's waiting for you in the storeroom where all the existing Christmas stuff is, as well as the boxes you brought down with you. She's keen to get started.'

'So am I.' Anything to keep her mind off her growing awareness of Oliver.

But a room full of Christmas? How would she cope without giving away the game that she was in fact a bah-humbug Scrooge? *Stick to the script*, she reminded herself. *And step into the role of someone who loves everything about Christmas.* She needed to pretend to be the person she'd been before the night of that fatal car crash.

She took a step nearer to Oliver. It brought her whispering-distance close. She was again dizzyingly aware of his warm, spicy and very male scent. It was a mix of some undoubtedly expensive aftershave with a hint of something uniquely him.

'Wish me luck with Edith,' she murmured.

'I'll make very sure I don't say anything controversial about my beloved boyfriend.' She knew there were people in the foyer watching them, some of them most likely guests. She turned up the volume. 'Shall I see you later?' she said as she leaned up to press a kiss on his cheek, then trailed a finger down it in a proprietorially girlfriend manner.

'Of course,' he said. He caught her hand in his and pressed a kiss on it, playing his role to perfection. 'I won't be there for lunch. We'll meet for dinner.' Even that light kiss on her hand felt good.

*Too good.*

Dinner? Of course it would be expected that they'd have dinner together. Would that happen every night? If she was really his girlfriend, of course it would. Breakfast, too. She'd be seeking any moment to be alone with her hot, gorgeous boyfriend, whose very closeness sent tremors of awareness coursing through her.

'Text me if anything untoward comes up I should know about,' he said. 'We may need script amendments as we go along.'

A script. It was a good reminder of this crazy scheme she'd got caught up in. Both she and Oliver were essentially playing roles in a Christmas play. That kiss, however, had not felt like play-acting. Unless Oliver was a *very* good actor. She realised how very little she knew about him apart from the personal memory of a boy from sixteen years ago. A boy she'd never been able to forget. And she realised she wanted to know a lot more.

He took her to meet Edith in a storeroom behind the kitchens in the back end of the hotel, in the staff-only areas where guests were not permitted, so she could seriously start work. He had things to do, places to go, Oliver said with a grin before making his escape. Marissa watched his retreating back and felt suddenly alone and unprepared to deal with his grandmother.

The room smelled faintly of Christmas: the lingering scent of pine leaves and pine cones, a hint of dusty potpourri, the leftover waxy trace of perfumed candles. Marissa had to swallow against a sudden rush of nausea at the thought of the terrors of Christmas past and her fear for Christmas future. She took a deep, steadying breath and pasted on a smile for Edith's benefit.

Again, she wondered what on earth she'd got herself into. Yet, to be able to help Caity at a time of great need for her friend made it worth it. And, she could not deny it, there was a bonus in the totally unexpected chance to see again that man she'd had such a huge crush on when she'd been a teenager.

Edith greeted Marissa with delight but, thank heaven, no risqué references to her love life with Oliver. She asked after Caity and was pleased with Marissa's report on her friend's continued good health while on hospital bed rest.

'Caity didn't mention to me that Oliver was dating a friend of hers,' Edith said with narrowed eyes.

When it came to clichés, 'thinking on her feet' now came to mind. 'That's because we didn't tell her,' Marissa said. 'The Pierce Group is her client. We didn't want to make things awkward for her. Besides, you know how private Oliver is. I'm the same. Our relationship is too new and too precious for us to want to go public with it.' The words tripped quite happily off her tongue, much as she'd rehearsed them with Oliver.

'I guessed as soon as I saw you. Your chemistry is so obvious,' Edith said.

Chemistry? Is that what had fuelled that incredible kiss? Was it chemistry that had fired the intensity of her teenage crush on the same man? Marissa was too taken aback to reply to the woman who fancied herself as her future grandmother-in-law. 'Er...yes,' was all she could manage in reply. This conversation was suddenly heading way off script.

The older woman continued. 'You know how pleased I am about you being together and I respect your need for privacy. It's just that Oliver hasn't had an easy life and I do want him to be happy. As happy with the right person as I was with Charles. We had our ups and downs, of course we did, but we were always there for each other. That's a great comfort through life.'

All Marissa could manage to choke out was, 'That's lovely.'

*She couldn't do this.*

How could she possibly do her job properly when all Oliver's grandmother seemed to want to talk about was Marissa's *relationship* with her grandson?

Edith chuckled. 'That's *lovely*, you say. But you've already told me you don't want to talk about you and Oliver. And as I want to keep on your right side, I'll butt out.'

*Please do!*

But Edith was relentless. 'I just want to be sure, my dear, that you know where I stand.'

'I most certainly do,' said Marissa, stifling the urge to laugh.

It was clear that Edith loved her grandson just as much as he loved her, and each was working in their own way to make the other happy. Marissa appreciated that. If she wasn't stuck in the middle of it, she would appreciate it even more. Still, she could do this job standing on her head, and the intrigue of the fake dating made it entertaining and edgy.

Edith showed her where the containers of heirloom tree ornaments, lights, staircase swags, buntings and Christmas linens had been placed, all brought down from the attics from where they spent the rest of the year.

'Some of the glass tree decorations go right back to when Charles was a little boy, living here with his parents, long before we turned the house into a hotel. We don't always put them up and, when we do, they're on a small tree in our private residence.' She sighed. 'I don't think I'll bother this year. Not on my own. The five hotel trees in the guest areas will be enough.'

'Are you sure?' Marissa said. 'I'm here to help with everything Christmas.'

Edith patted her on the hand. 'Thank you for

your kind offer, my dear. But I'll pass. For this year anyway.'

Marissa thought about where she herself would be next Christmas. On that Balinese island, for sure. On her own and loving it.

The Christmas trees were to be placed in the guest areas, including the foyer, the living room, dining room, reading room and in the living room of the converted barn.

Edith pointed out that the decorations for each room had been packed together and put in clearly marked boxes and wooden packing crates. Marissa knew that from Caity's detailed handover document, but she had to check for herself to be sure. Attention to detail was all important.

Some of the ornaments and decorations were packed in very old suitcases that harked back to the golden age of sea travel to Europe, America and far-flung destinations of the Commonwealth before air travel took over. The suitcases were plastered with overlapping labels emblazoned with the names of grand ocean liners and stamped 'First Class.' Port labels told of voyages to destinations such as Marseille, Naples and Athens; transatlantic crossings to New York; further afield to exotic destinations like Bombay and Sydney, and back home to Dover.

She found the labels fascinating, telling a story of a glamorous era long gone for Oliver's wealthy family. She'd love to know more about their history. But now wasn't the time to delve into that. Perhaps it might be a good conversation starter over dinner with Oliver.

There were also the boxes of new product she'd brought with her in the van—including custom-made Christmas crackers. She cut open the box closest to her, using a utility knife with a retractable blade from the table nearby. She had, of course, inspected all the products at the designer's London headquarters to ensure the quality was up to scratch for her discerning clients. But she'd inspect them again for any possible damage sustained in transit.

She referred to her tablet. 'Soon, the team of contract staff will arrive,' she said. 'And the trees are due to be delivered from the Christmas tree farm later today. We have five trees of varying sizes for each of the five main public rooms. The trees will be stored outside in the barn and then brought inside when required.'

'We have the same helpers most years, so they know what to do,' Edith said.

Marissa had also engaged a professional

interior designer with expertise in Christmas trees. Andy Gable had made a lucrative career out of decorating Christmas trees for private homes and hotels, department stores in both London and New York, along with many different magazines and catalogues. Marissa marvelled at how he made each tree so unique to that job. His job—his vocation, he called it—allowed him to take summers off to travel the world. Marissa had called him to ask for tree-decorating advice. To her delight, an unexpected cancellation had given him a free four days to help her out at Longfield Manor. He'd be arriving first thing the next day.

Caity had recruited fresh blood, too—a team of local university students on their Christmas break.

*Strong young people who will be safe on ladders, unlike some of the regular elderly helpers.*

That was what Caity had written in her notes. Marissa smiled to herself as she read the notes but didn't read them out loud. She wasn't in any way ageist; in fact, she respected the knowledge and wisdom older people brought with them. But the fact remained that decorating a hotel of this size, with massive rooms and high ceilings, would be hard, physical work. Especially within this tight time frame.

She turned to Edith. 'I'm going to say goodbye and pop up to my room and change into jeans.' She'd dressed in business clothes for her first meeting with the clients, but now she needed to dress for hard work.

There was a guest lift, but she enjoyed climbing that magnificent staircase. For a moment, she imagined how it would be to be holding up voluminous long skirts of a bygone age as she manoeuvred the steps. Once in her room, she changed into jeans, a long-sleeved T-shirt and sturdy sneakers. Nothing scruffy, all designer, in keeping with the high-end hotel. Her role as event planner was a supervisory one. However, she had never been one to stand back if hands-on help was needed.

She pulled her hair back tighter into the ponytail; she hadn't realised stray wisps had come free during her enthusiastic kiss with Oliver. It was a battle to keep the luxuriant waves sleek. She looked in the mirror to check her make-up and touched up her lipstick where it had been kissed off. A shiver of pleasure ran through her as she remembered how good his kiss had felt. How was that possible when it had been with the man who had been so awful to her as a teenager?

Today Oliver Pierce had called her lovely. He had called her beautiful. And he'd sounded like he'd meant it. A stark departure from what had happened in the past. Back when he was sixteen and named Oliver Hughes, her friend Samantha's brother Toby had asked Oliver what he thought about his sister's friend. The boys were sitting on a sofa in Samantha's family's living room, where they'd been playing games on their consoles. They didn't know she could overhear them from the other side of the open door into the room.

*Eavesdroppers rarely hear good things about themselves*, her mother had told her. How true that had been back then.

Oliver certainly hadn't had anything flattering to say about her infatuated, self-conscious fourteen-year-old self. Neither had Toby, whom she had always liked up until then.

That day Toby had kicked off the critique by pointing out how flat-chested she was—true, she hadn't developed significant curves for another two years—how gawky—she hadn't grown into her long limbs yet then, either—and how she giggled too much—also unfortunately true, especially in the company of boys other than her brother.

It was such a cruel summing-up for a girl who was just beginning to find her place in a world where she had believed she might have something to offer. Where boys had become interesting rather than nuisances. Her heart had shattered when Oliver had agreed with Toby's assessments. Before that, she had never thought she was ugly, but when she'd seen herself through his eyes…she'd felt it.

Then Oliver had asked Toby, 'What's with those caterpillars crawling across the top of her face?'

Toby had sniggered. 'Marissa's monobrow, you mean.'

Toby had laughed and Oliver had joined in, too. Laughing at *her.*

She had been super-self-conscious about her eyebrows. Hearing the boys' laughter, she'd thought she would die of shame and embarrassment. But she couldn't crawl away, or they would have known she'd been there listening to them on the other side of the door. And for them to know she'd heard their mocking laughter would have made her feel even worse.

Thankfully, the boys had then headed off to the kitchen in search of food, and she'd crept away and gone home, even though she'd been expected to stay for lunch with the family and Toby's friend. There had still been two days left of their half-term break but she'd made excuses not to go back to Samantha's house again. Not until obnoxious Toby and his equally obnoxious friend had gone back to their boarding school. Oliver had thankfully never visited again, and she had avoided Toby every holiday he'd been home.

After the pain and rejection she'd felt from that overheard conversation, that cruel laughter, she'd been determined to do something about her bothersome eyebrows.

Back then, her eyebrows had been bushy and black, and stray hairs had met in the middle above her nose. She'd hated those eyebrows but her mother had forbidden her to do anything about them, apart from the most gentle plucking. 'You can ruin your eyebrows for life if you pluck too much,' she'd warned.

So she'd saved up her pocket money and her babysitting money. Then she'd defied her mother by taking the bus to Knightsbridge to visit an eyebrow clinic reputed to be the best in London. Those errant eyebrows had been plucked, threaded and waxed into the elegant arches that today framed her eyes. She was still absolutely vigilant about keeping them that way.

Was that why Oliver hadn't recognised her? There was a curious satisfaction in knowing that he now found that skinny, gawky, mono-browed girl beautiful. That his kiss indicated he was attracted to her. But now her relationship with the client had veered into the personal, should she remind him that they'd met before? She still wasn't sure there would be any point to such a revelation.

# CHAPTER SIX

BUSINESS HAD KEPT Oliver confined to his office for most of the day. It was Christmas in his London hotels, with no vacancies across the three properties, which meant there were a lot of calls on staff. There were guests who'd come to London for shopping, London people who wanted to spend Christmas being pampered at a hotel, travellers from other countries wanting to enjoy a legendary English Christmas. He should really be in London himself, but he had excellent managers and for the moment he was putting Granny and Longfield Manor first. Thankfully, much of what he needed to do could be done remotely.

However, busy as he was, he found his thoughts straying often to Marissa. He was looking forward to having dinner with her. Not in his private residence—to be alone with her would be a test of his endurance as he definitely wanted to kiss her again—but rather at the hotel dining room. He wanted to get to know her better.

He'd had time to think about the fake-girl-friend scenario he had proposed. Where had that idea come from? Making quick decisions and taking risks in business had certainly paid off for him. But when it came to his personal life, he didn't do rash, impulsive things like asking a stranger to pretend to be his girl-friend. Or to suggest they practise kissing because all he'd been able to think about since meeting her was kissing her.

Yet, the scene in his office that morning had seemed so right. He recalled his fears for his grandmother, so caught up in her delu-sion. Marissa, an acquaintance of—what had it been then? An hour?—unwittingly caught up in it, unaware of the sad backstory of his family, so willing to be kind and thoughtful about Granny. This empathic woman seemed aware of his pain at his loss because she had suffered loss, too.

And it was working. Granny had a definite spring to her step that had been missing for a long time, even before Grandpa had died. Sim-ply because she believed he had a girlfriend. No. Not just any girlfriend. Marissa. A girl she thought he must be in love with if he'd brought her home for Christmas.

He was so grateful to Marissa. He would find some acceptable way to reward her when this was all over. After he had gracefully 'broken up' with her. For the first time since coming up with his scheme, he felt a twinge of concern. If Granny was so obsessed with Marissa, how would she feel about having to say goodbye to her? Yet, no one would be surprised. Oliver did not do long-term relationships, and everyone knew that.

There wasn't much daylight left given that at this time of year sunset was at 4 p.m. and, as Oliver liked to take a walk around the gardens while it was still light, he decided to take a break. He pulled on his coat, hat and gloves as he headed outside. The sky was clear and blue and the air distinctly chilly. A heavy frost was predicted. But it was so good to be outside. He headed past the walled garden, enclosed within high walls of the same stone as the main buildings, a suntrap where spring came earlier than for the rest of the garden.

As he walked past, heading for the wild garden area, he saw that the iron gate was pushed open. For a moment he didn't recognise Marissa, in jeans, a puffer coat and scarf wrapped high to her chin. 'You startled me,' she said. 'I was taking the chance to get some fresh air.' She indicated the garden behind her. 'What a wonderful private garden.'

'Granny's pride and joy,' he said. 'It was originally the kitchen garden to supply vegetables and fruit to the house. In the old days, they also grew herbs for medicinal purposes. We still grow herbs there for the restaurant. And although it's now mainly a flower garden, you might have noticed fruit trees espaliered onto the walls.'

She laughed. 'I don't know much at all about gardening. Or what *espaliered* means. But I sensed a feeling of peace and fulfilment in there. In winter it has a certain bare beauty. It must be awesome covered in snow. But in summer, it must be delightful to sit on one of those stone benches and contemplate.'

'Granny grows lavender and roses and other scented plants there, because she thinks that way, too. She chooses plants with texture and others that attract butterflies. There's a fountain, too, emptied now so it doesn't freeze. She calls it her sensory garden.'

'Not that you get much time for sitting in there contemplating, I should imagine. Not with your hotel empire.'

'You're right. I don't.' But as a young boy he'd liked to hide in there behind the walls at the end of the school holidays, hoping they wouldn't be able to find him to take him back to boarding school. 'I'm walking down through the lawns to the wild garden if you'd like to join me.'

'Wild garden?' she said as she fell into step beside him. He didn't feel he had to hold her hand as there wasn't anyone to see them. Strangely enough, though, an inner compulsion made him want to reach out for her hand. Instead, he kept his hands firmly shoved into his coat pockets.

'An area that's been sown as a natural meadow. It attracts butterflies and wildlife like hedgehogs. It was my grandfather's idea. The Manor gardens are…were…his passion. He told me it was difficult for him to deal with strangers living in his home when they first opened it as a hotel. So the gardens became his domain.'

'How did you feel?'

'I don't remember it any other way,' he said. 'Guests tended to be nice to a little boy, so I was fine with it. Sometimes I got to play with children staying here and I liked that.'

'Liked it enough to become a hotel tycoon yourself when you grew up?'

'There's that,' he said, not wishing to be drawn in to further conversation about his childhood. Or the years spent relentlessly proving himself as a success in his own right.

'It must have been an amazing place to grow up in,' she said, looking around her at the formal gardens and the lawn that ran down to a rise from where the sea was visible.

'It was,' Oliver said. Which was why he would do everything in his power to keep Longfield Manor in the family. 'I hear you're doing brilliantly with the Christmas decorations.'

Marissa smiled. 'A report from Edith, no doubt? She's been great. No interrogation about possible birth dates of the great-grandchildren.'

Oliver laughed. 'I'm glad to hear that.'

'Seriously, she's just letting me get on with my job supervising the crew while she does her own thing with the family heirlooms.'

'I love Christmas at Longfield Manor,' Oliver said, looking around him. 'The happiest memories of my life are here and the happiest of all are from Christmas. I hope you're enjoying taking part in it.'

'About that.' Marissa came to a halt next to him. 'Before you go any further, there's something you need to know about me.'

Oliver frowned. What could possibly have brought that serious expression to her face? 'Fire away,' he said.

'I don't celebrate Christmas,' she said bluntly. 'In answer to your question, while I'm enjoying the job and liking the people I'm working with, Christmas itself leaves me cold.'

Oliver was so taken aback, he struggled for the right words. 'Is it your religion?'

She shook her head. 'Nothing to do with that. You spoke about memories... Well, my memories of Christmas aren't that great. My most recent ones, anyway.'

'But...but everyone loves Christmas,' he said.

'Many people don't celebrate Christmas,' she said. 'And there are people who find it stressful, or feel lonely and left out at this time of year.'

'Point taken. But you...?' Did she have an unhappy childhood? Abusive parents? He realised how very little he knew about her.

'I have my reasons, and I don't want to talk about them,' she said, looking at the ground. 'But I thought you needed to know why I don't wax enthusiastic about Christmas. That doesn't stop me appreciating the beauty of the decorations we're putting up or the deliciousness of the menu. This Scrooge will do as good a job for you as any Christmas fan, I promise.'

'I appreciate that,' he said. 'But why did a self-professed Scrooge take on the job?'

'To help out Caity. She's my best friend.'

'Does she know how you feel about Christmas?'

'Yes.'

'So why did she choose you to replace her?'

'Because she trusts me to do every bit as good a job as she would to make this Christmas special for Longfield Manor.'

'Did you resent coming here and immersing yourself in Christmas?' He didn't like that thought at all.

'Not for a minute,' she said. 'And I'm enjoying being here.' She looked up at him and her eyes danced. 'Including pretending to be your girlfriend. That adds an edge to the job to make it even more enjoyable. Everyone is very interested in us, by the way. I've had to field lots of questions.' She put up her hand. 'Don't worry, I've stuck to the script.'

'I've been in my office for most of the day and have managed to avoid any questioning. Although both Cecil and Priya made a few less than subtle hints that they were interested in our story.'

'I think the staff might feel it would be out of place to question you about your personal life. You can seem…forbidding.'

He bristled. 'I'm the boss. It comes with the role.'

'Of course. But remember you're meant to be madly in love. At the mention of your lover's name, you might want to soften a tad. Maybe show a hint of a goofy grin.'

He drew himself up to his full height. 'Me? A goofy grin? I don't do goofy.'

'You could try.' A mischievous smile tilted her lips and exposed that delightful dimple.

Oliver gave an exaggerated grin and he rolled his eyes at the ridiculousness of it.

She laughed. 'That's terrible and you know it. If you can't do goofy you need to try at least a gentling of your expression. You have resting stern face.'

She took a step closer to him and walked the fingers of her right hand up his arm to his shoulder. He was hyperaware of her touch, of her rose-and-vanilla scent.

'Now, look down at me with the dazed and besotted expression of a man in love. A man so in love he has brought a woman to his childhood home for the very first time.'

Oliver tried. And tried again. But he knew he was only achieving a grimace. He shrugged.

'Okay, call that a fail,' said Marissa. 'Why not try to picture someone who you were in love with and recall how you felt when you looked into her face.'

Oliver swallowed hard. 'I… I can't do that,' he said. He shook his head. 'I just can't do it.'

'Because you're not good at imagining?' Marissa paused. 'Or…or because you've never been in love?'

'Right the second time,' he managed to choke out. He saw from her expression that perhaps this wasn't an answer that reflected well on a thirty-two-year-old man.

'You've never been in love?' She sounded incredulous.

'Never. Attracted. Infatuated. Interested. But no, not in love.'

'Oh,' she said with a frown. 'But you're handsome, rich, nice. Women must be falling over themselves to date you.'

She called him *nice*? That wasn't a word often used to describe him. Oddly enough, he liked it. 'True,' he said without arrogance. After all, it was the truth. 'But that doesn't mean I've fallen in love with any of them.'

'I see,' she said. 'I wasn't expecting that. No wonder you can't fake it, then.'

'What about you?'

'Have I ever been in love?' Her perfectly shaped eyebrows rose.

'Yes.' He found himself holding his breath for her answer.

'Well, yes. A couple of times. But it didn't work out either time. Then there was—' She stopped.

'There was...' he prompted.

She didn't meet his eyes. 'Another time. When I was a young teenager I fell wildly, irrationally in love with a boy who...who didn't even notice me. I...guess I could put that down to infatuation. Kid stuff.' Her mouth set into a tight line at what seemed to be a painful memory. She opened her mouth as if to say something else but evidently decided against it.

'Infatuation can come easily,' he said, for want of saying anything more meaningful.

Had he consciously resisted love? He'd been so rejected by his parents he could see how that could have put a lock on his feelings. Or had his determination to succeed as a hotelier blocked anything and anyone that could get in the way? Could he have grown to love Sonya if given the chance? Or had what he'd felt for her been classified as infatuation?

He started to walk again and Marissa walked beside him. It was getting colder by the minute and her breath fogged in the sharp, late-afternoon air.

'What about someone else you loved?' she asked. 'We've got quite an audience back at the Manor. Can you manage to conjure up feelings to give authenticity to our mock-relationship?'

He realised the only people who had loved him unconditionally and whom he had loved in return were his grandparents. But that was a very different kind of love. And it was that love for them that was behind his determination to ensure the happiest of Christmases for his grandmother. Marissa was talking about romantic love, something entirely foreign and unfamiliar to him.

She stopped walking and he came to a halt near her. 'What about a pet? A dog or cat or horse? I adored my cat. She was old when I inherited her along with my flat from my godmother, so I didn't have her for long. But I loved her so much. If I think about her, I think love would show in my eyes.'

He stared at her. 'What? You think it would work if I called up the love I had for my dog?'

He laughed. 'Seriously? You want me to fake a goofy grin with memories of my dog? Who I did love a lot, by the way. He was actually Grandpa's dog, but he was mine when I was here.'

'Er, it's a thought,' she said.

He turned her around to face him. 'So to evoke the required emotion, I look into your face and imagine you're Rufus, my black Labrador?'

Her eyes widened, she bit her lip and she laughed—an awkward, half-speed kind of laugh. 'Not one of my best ideas. Sorry. Scratch that one.'

She was obviously embarrassed, and he didn't want her to feel worse by saying anything else. Although the memory of the best-ever dog Rufus, who'd lived a good long life before succumbing to old age, did warm his heart. Grandpa had been feeling his years at the time, and they'd decided as a family not to get another puppy. But one day, if he ever settled down, he knew he'd want a black Labrador.

He and Marissa turned and walked back to the house. He was disconcerted to find that when he looked into her face, he couldn't conjure up images of past infatuations or even women he'd liked. Because the only face he was remotely interested in seeing was Marissa's own.

He also realised that with her talk of goofy grins and love and infatuation and dogs, she had diverted the conversation quite away from herself and her loathing of Christmas. What had happened there?

# CHAPTER SEVEN

OLIVER SAT AT his personal table in the hotel dining room. The staff knew it was his exclusively for the times he chose not to dine in his private quarters. Some of the guests gave him discreet nods, but most of them would have no idea he was the grandson of the owners of Longfield Manor and owner of the most fashionable hotels in London.

That gave him the opportunity to check on service. Every night he'd sat here, he'd seen exemplary service and high levels of guest satisfaction. His table, laid with the same fine but not fussy linen and china as the other tables, was in a secluded corner of the large, welcoming room. A fire blazed in the massive medieval fireplace at one end, emanating warmth and cosiness.

Oliver was dining here tonight with Marissa. He was early and she was spot on time. As she stepped tentatively into the room, looking around her—looking for *him*—he caught his breath. She looked sensational in a black dress that hugged her curves and ended above her knees. Her jeans and trousers had hinted at long, shapely legs, and his guess was now confirmed by the dress and sky-high black stilettos. Yet, her look was subtle, in keeping with her role as a consultant. If she hadn't been pretending to be his girlfriend, might she have kept her hair tied back from her face? Instead, she'd let it tumble below her shoulders, thick and luxuriant, glinting with highlights from the chandeliers. How would it feel to run his hands through it?

She spoke a few words to the maître d' who, with a flourish, led her towards Oliver's table. As she approached, Oliver got up to greet her. The maître d' made a fuss of her, pushing in her chair, making sure she was comfortable, shaking out her table napkin onto her lap. The older man had been with the hotel for years, and Oliver recognised the gleam of speculation as he sat his *girlfriend* opposite him.

Her blue eyes looked even bluer, outlined with dark make-up, and her lips were defined with deep red lipstick. He was often in proximity to beautiful, glamorous and famous women as The Pierce Group hotels were the current cool places to be seen in London. But not one of those women could hold a candle to Marissa. His heart started to thud. He couldn't let her know how attracted he was to her. That wasn't part of the charade.

'You look very beautiful,' he said slowly, his gaze taking in every detail of her appearance. The neckline of her dress revealed the swell of her breasts, an amethyst pendant nestling between them.

*Lucky necklace.*

As her boyfriend it would be *expected* of him to compliment her. But just being him, Oliver Pierce single guy, he found he *wanted* to tell her how beautiful she was.

'Thank you.' She smiled. That cute dimple was a well-placed punctuation mark to her lovely face. 'I thought I'd better up my game if I'm to pass muster as your girlfriend.'

'You have no cause for concern in that regard,' he said hoarsely.

*She was super-hot.*

'As long as you approve.'

'I approve,' he said wholeheartedly.

Her eyes widened. 'Well done!'

He frowned. 'Well done?'

'That look. I see emotion. I see affection. I see everything we discussed earlier. You've got it.' Her eyes narrowed. 'Are you channelling your feelings towards your dog Rufus? Is it because I'm wearing black?'

Oliver laughed. 'Of course not. I'm just acting. Playing a role.' What had she seen in his eyes? What had he revealed about how he felt seeing her so sexy and vivacious?

'Well, Academy award for you,' she said. 'There should be no trouble convincing people we're in a real relationship.'

He didn't like to say that his reaction to her had nothing to do with love but everything to do with lust. There could be no doubt he liked her more with every minute he spent with her. But liking someone plus being attracted to her did not equate to love—even the stirrings of love. Not that he and love and Marissa had anything to do with it. Would ever have anything to do with it. This was all pretend.

He indicated the menus on the table. 'Shall we start with a cocktail?'

'A mocktail for me, please. I never drink alcohol while I'm working.'

'You're not working now.'

'Aren't I?' She leaned across the table close to him and lowered her voice to a murmur. 'I'm on girlfriend duty, remember.'

'Point taken.'

She was doing the extra job for which she'd refused payment. And so far, she was doing it brilliantly. But even though he'd devised the whole scheme, something started to rankle with him. This gorgeous woman—more than one head in the restaurant had turned to admire her as she'd made her way across the room to his table—equated spending time with him as a chore. Perhaps he was the one who needed to lift his game.

He ordered mocktails for them both.

Marissa held the folder in her hand without looking at the carefully curated menu, which highlighted local produce. 'What a treat,' she said. 'This room is amazing. And the food sounds fabulous. I'm going to have a hard time deciding what to eat.'

'The food is excellent, even if I say so myself,' he said. 'But you haven't read the menu yet.'

'I don't need to. I had a quick meeting with the head chef today about the Christmas menus. He ran me through the menu choices for tonight. My mouth was watering by the time he'd got through the appetisers.'

The good-looking French chef was a notorious flirt, and Oliver was surprised at the sudden flare of jealousy that seared through him at the thought of Jean Paul turning on the charm for Marissa. He dismissed it immediately as foolishness. Besides, he knew Jean Paul was devoted to his wife and two young sons.

'Jean Paul is an excellent chef. We are fortunate to have him with us.'

'He told me how much he loves the lifestyle here for his family.'

Good. No flirting with Oliver's *girlfriend*, then. Jean Paul's job was safe. Oliver gritted his teeth. He couldn't believe he'd entertained that thought for even a second. He wasn't a jealous guy. And Marissa wasn't really his girlfriend. As a hotelier, if he had to choose between a highly regarded and sought-after chef and a woman, the woman wouldn't even get a look-in.

*But if that woman was Marissa?*

He couldn't go there, and was shocked at the direction his thoughts had taken him.

Marissa looked across to Oliver, darkly handsome in a charcoal-grey shirt. He'd obviously shaved to keep the stubble on his chin at bay. He must be a twice-a-day shave man. She'd read somewhere that meant high levels of testosterone. A shiver of awareness ran through her at the thought.

Why did he have to be so darn handsome? And such good company. Keeping up the fake-girlfriend thing in front of other people was stressful; there was no doubt about that. She had to be on the alert not to let the mask slip with an inadvertent comment or response that would reveal they were lying—there was no other word for it—about their relationship. Yet, when she was alone with him, she felt relaxed and enjoyed their conversations. Not to mention she was still wildly attracted to him. Good looks aside, he seemed so different from when he'd been sixteen. Did her concept of him, forged in teenage angst, no longer fit the man he was now? Twice today she'd started to tell him about their past acquaintanceship but twice couldn't find the courage to continue. But did it matter?

They ordered from the menu. For a starter, she chose the wild mushroom tart followed by the trout with almond butter. Oliver ordered the lime-cured salmon and the herbed fillet of beef. She'd been very impressed with Jean Paul, the chef, and wanted to see if the meals tasted as good as they sounded. Caity had, of course, already done a tasting of the proposed Christmas menus along with Edith, so that was one less thing to worry about.

Oliver sat back in his chair. 'I have to keep reminding myself that I only met you for the first time this morning.'

*Not quite the first time.*

'I feel as though I've known you for longer. As if we've put a week's worth of getting to know you into one day.'

'Funny, I was thinking the same thing. I guess it's because we had to accelerate the process to make it believable that we're a couple.'

'That must be it,' he said, not sounding totally convinced.

'It makes our relationship seem more authentic and that's all that counts, isn't it?'

She wondered if there was any chance of a continuing friendship or acquaintanceship of any kind between her and Oliver, or even with Edith whom, despite her outrageous comments, she had already become quite fond of. But that was unlikely, she thought. Although if she did a good job of this—of Christmas, of faking it—she could at least ensure Caity's ongoing business with The Pierce Group. And that was the sole reason she was here, wasn't it?

No, after pretend kissing that had seemed only too real, it would be impossible to see Oliver again after this was over and act normally.

She would probably never see him again. And she wasn't sure how she felt about that.

'You have very good online reviews for Longfield Manor,' she said.

'You looked them up?'

'Before I got here.'

'There are many other letters and testimonials, too, from guests who aren't into the internet,' he said.

'That must be very gratifying.'

'It is, especially for Granny. A lot of guests feel a personal connection to this place.'

'My favourite review was one that said the hotel was like a home away from home, only a very posh home.'

Oliver laughed. 'I like that. It's just what we want them to think. The home-away-from-home bit, I mean.'

'Posh without being intimidating,' she said.

Again, she thought about what it must be like to grow up in surroundings like this. And how clever his grandparents had been to turn around their fortunes by transforming their home into a hotel.

'Of course it's posh but I don't think of it that way. It's home.'

An exceedingly posh home. 'How long have your family lived here?'

'Since the early nineteenth century. Going back to then, my ancestors were industrialists who cashed in on the railway boom. No blue blood but plenty of money and quick to seize an opportunity. They had good taste in real estate. I don't remember it but, by all accounts, the London townhouse was also very grand. I know my mother was devastated when it was sold.'

'And now there are your hotels in London. It must be in the blood.'

'Perhaps,' he said with a slight smile.

'Talking of posh, I loved the old suitcases that store some of the decorations. Your ancestors were very well travelled.'

'They're amazing relics, aren't they? From an era where travel was leisurely, not just trying to get from A to B as quickly as possible.'

'In those days it would have taken weeks to get to India or Australia.'

'I would be too impatient for that,' he said.

'Me, too,' she said. 'Have you travelled much?'

'Not as much as I'd have liked to. Establishing my business has always been my priority. Travel has mostly involved staying in other company's hotels to see how they worked and to size up the competition.'

'So you're a workaholic?'

'And proud of it.'

She would be proud, too, looking at what he had achieved. She wondered what motivated him to be so driven. His childhood, perhaps? She didn't dare ask.

Their meals arrived and the food lived up to its descriptions and more. It was so delicious she wanted to savour the taste, rather than chat. Jean Paul was a genius. Living at Longfield Manor for another six days was not going to be a hardship.

'Pudding?' asked Oliver.

'Not tonight, thank you, tempting as that menu is,' she said. 'I had an early start followed by a big day. And my Christmas tree designer will be arriving early in the morning tomorrow so I should turn in soon.'

'A Christmas tree designer. Is that a thing?'

'It is for Andy. He's made a career of it and he's in great demand. I was only able to book him as he had a last-minute cancellation because of a fire on the site where he was scheduled to be working.'

'Lucky us,' said Oliver.

'Do I detect a note of sarcasm there?'

'Certainly not. I respect any designer. My hotels wouldn't be the successes they are without the talented designers who work with me. They excel at Christmas trees and make sure everything they do fits with the overall design vision for the interiors.'

'Whereas here there's a wonderful mish-mash of old and new, family heirlooms and the new decorations Caity commissioned to be unique to Longfield Manor.'

'You're okay working with them? The Christmas decorations, I mean.'

She felt her expression shut down as it did when Christmas was mentioned. 'Of course,' she said.

Oliver paused before speaking as if he was carefully choosing his words. 'Is there a reason you don't celebrate Christmas?'

'Not one I care to discuss,' she said, aware of the chill that had crept into her voice.

Why had he ruined such a thoroughly pleasant evening by bringing up her aversion to Christmas? Did he expect that she'd happily spill some answers? She could predict what would come next if she did so. Inevitably, the person she'd confided in would try to change her mind. Why would Oliver be any different? This whole place, him included, was happy-clappy about Christmas.

She got up from the table. 'Thank you for a

marvellous dinner. But I really need to be getting up to my room.'

Oliver rose from his chair. 'Let me escort you.'

'I can manage on my own, thank you,' she said.

He came around to her side of the table. 'I'm your boyfriend, remember?' he said in a low voice.

'Sorry. How could I forget?' she murmured as she put her hand mock-possessively on his arm.

*Just don't forget even for a second that this—he—isn't real.*

Marissa wasn't sure what to say as Oliver walked beside her up that magnificent staircase to her room on the first floor. There was a small guest elevator, but she was determined not to ever take it and miss out on an opportunity to take the stairs and think about the grand past of the manor house.

In silence he walked down the corridor beside her, until they reached her room. Marissa pulled the old-fashioned brass key to the room out of her purse. 'Here I am,' she said, her voice coming out as an awkward croak. Why had he asked her about Christmas? They'd been getting on so well.

'Room eight,' Oliver said. 'That sounds so mundane, doesn't it? When my grandparents started the hotel, Granny had the idea she'd name each room after a Dorset wildflower.'

'A lovely idea.'

'She thought so, too. She started off with Honeysuckle, Snowdrop and Primrose. But when it came to Butterwort and Bogbean she decided to pass on the idea.'

'Seriously?'

'That's how she tells it.'

'The Bogbean Room wouldn't have quite the same cachet, would it?' Marissa laughed. But Oliver just smiled.

'You have a delightful laugh,' he said.

'Do I?' she said.

'Your face lights up. And your eyes, well, they dance. I never knew what that expression meant until I saw you laugh.'

'Oh,' she said, flushing, not sure what else to say.

She looked up to him—even in her high heels he was taller—seeking words for an answer that never came. His expression was serious; his green eyes darkened. She was conscious of her own breathing, the accelerated beat of her heart, his stillness. 'Marissa,' he finally said, her name hanging in the air of the silent, empty corridor.

'I appreciate so much what you're doing for me, for my family. Especially since you don't celebrate Christmas. If I get it right, you don't actually *like* Christmas.'

She put up her hand to stop him. 'Oliver, I—'

'The whys and wherefores of that are totally your own business. I'm sorry I brought it up over dinner and I won't ask you again.'

She didn't drop her gaze from his face, sensed his genuine remorse.

'Thank you,' she said.

She couldn't stop looking up at him, drawn to him as if mesmerised. Her breath came faster at the intensity of his gaze. He traced a finger down the side of her face, a simple gesture that felt like an intimate caress. She reached up to take his hand, not sure whether she meant to run her tongue along his finger or push it away. Instead, she laid her own fingers across his, keeping him close.

Then his mouth was on hers and he was kissing her. There was no need for him to kiss her, no witnesses in that corridor who could attest that their relationship was genuine. There was nothing pretend or fake about this kiss and she should push him away. But she didn't want to stop. She wanted to kiss him, to kiss him hard.

*To kiss him for real.*

She returned the pressure of his mouth with hers and wound her arms around his neck. He pulled her closer and deepened the kiss. Desire pulsed through her. She wanted him. He wanted her, too, she could tell.

She wanted more than kisses. When she thought of it, she'd always wanted him—right back to when she'd been fourteen years old. Back then her longing for him had gone no further than the hope of exciting, sweet kisses and cuddles. Her virginal imagination had taken her no further. Now her thoughts so easily took her to what would happen if she pushed her door open and they stumbled, kissing and caressing, into her room with the door slammed shut behind them.

There would be no going back.

Everything would change.

The game would be for real—and she would not come out the winner.

She broke away from the kiss, pushed him away, took a deep, steadying breath, felt her cheeks flushed. 'If we continue kissing like this we both know where it will lead us. And I don't want to go there. That's not part of the deal. To work with you after that would be so awkward.' She wanted him too much to play with the flickering flames of intense desire.

'We could make it work,' he said hoarsely.

'No,' she said, and he immediately let her go. 'I'm attracted to you. I think you know that. But I don't do one-night stands or casual flings.'

'Understood,' he said as he took a step back. She noted he didn't say he didn't do casual, either. But then that didn't surprise her. He'd made his stance on relationships very clear.

She wrapped her arms around her middle as if barricading herself. 'So far, we're doing well with the fake relationship for the sake of your grandmother. I'm happy to continue that. But now I want to say good-night, and when I see you tomorrow it should be as if this had never happened. Please.'

# CHAPTER EIGHT

AFTER A RESTLESS NIGHT, when sleep had proved elusive, Marissa was glad of the distraction provided by her friend Andy, the Christmas tree designer, and his visit to Longfield Manor. She and Andy had first worked together years ago when they were on staff at the same company.

Andy's full-on personality wouldn't allow time for regretful thoughts about Oliver. She was so drawn to him, the attraction so magnetic. Should she have invited him to her bed and taken the chance on something wonderful but ephemeral? Was she being overprotective of her feelings? On balance, she decided she'd made the right decision last night. It was hard enough to keep on an even keel surrounded by Christmas let alone being immersed in emotional angst if she went too far with Oliver. He had an immense power to hurt her. Even his thoughtless insults as a teenager had caused long-lasting pain.

She stood patiently by while Andy chastised her for not letting him go out to the Christmas tree farm to choose and cut the trees himself.

'I know you're Mr Perfectionist, and like total control over the tree,' she said. 'But this has all been a bit last-minute. I'm standing in for Caity,' she explained.

'I get it, you had to help Caity out,' Andy replied. 'And the bonus is the hot boss.' He made a lascivious face. 'How does he identify?'

'He. Him. Heterosexual.'

'You go, girl,' Andy said.

Marissa was about to totally deny any interest in the CEO of The Pierce Group. But she quickly pulled herself up. *No slips.* She was meant to be Oliver's girlfriend.

She smiled the fakest of smiles. 'We're together, actually.'

'Together as in *together*?'

'Yes. I'm dating him. Have been since early November. We met at—' There she went, over-embellishing. 'Never mind where we met.'

'Congratulations.'

Marissa couldn't resist adding something vaguely truthful. 'I'm keeping quiet about it as Oliver isn't…isn't into long-term relationships.'

'And you are?'

'One day, yes,' she said, surprising herself. She hadn't thought she was ready.

'And you don't want to put pressure on him?'

'No. It's not like that. I don't want to be embarrassed when it ends.'

'You pessimist! Is it good to anticipate the end when you've barely started?'

'Less painful that way when it doesn't work out,' she said.

It would end and end soon. *Because it wasn't real.* And already she knew she would be sad when she had to say goodbye to her fake boyfriend. In spite of her longtime grudge, she liked him.

'If you say so,' he said, not seeming convinced. 'Now, take me to the Christmas trees.'


Marissa was on her own in the reading room, a drawing room also called the quiet room. It was one of the smaller public rooms where guests were encouraged to take time out to read, listen to music through headphones, or even nap in the comfortable sofas and easy chairs. The beautifully proportioned room was decorated, as everywhere in Longfield Manor, with impeccable taste in traditional English country house style with Edith's unique twist on it.

Marissa stood on the jewel-toned Persian

carpet, just her and a Christmas tree, the smallest of the five trees to be placed around the hotel. Andy had started the decoration and had left strict instructions on the precise order in which to place each bauble, bead and star in exact colour combinations, a measured distance from the end of the branch.

It wasn't she who was meant to be actually dressing the tree with such precision. She wouldn't volunteer for the task in a million years. In fact, she'd only been in this room to introduce two of the temporary student staff to Andy and leave them to it. However, Andy had been so impressed with the students' design skills and willingness to learn, he'd spirited them away to assist him in dressing the tallest of the trees. That giant fir would tower in festive grandeur over the living room and be the star of the Christmas celebrations. He'd asked Marissa to watch the room and keep guests out until he returned with another team.

She was wearing black jeans and a smart textured jacket and she began to feel uncomfortable. The room was very warm, stuffy even, with a wood fire burning in the fireplace. Marissa hated the smell of pine needles. The scent from the tree pervaded the room, no matter how far she stood away from it. There was no escape from it. She put her hands to her head as it began to overwhelm her.

The sharp acrid smell of pine permeated her lungs, making her feel dizzy and disoriented. Her breath came in short gasps. She clutched on to the back of a high-backed chair. Nausea rose in her throat and she swallowed against it.

On Christmas Eve her parents had been transporting the Christmas tree home on the top of the car when the accident had happened. The pine needles had scattered all over the car, all over them. Afterwards, she and her brother, stricken by grief and disbelief, had wanted to see where it had happened. Pine needles and broken glass had been all over the ground where the car had left the road and smashed into a fence. When she collected her parents' possessions from the hospital, her mother's handbag had been full of the needles and they'd been scattered over her father's favourite tweed jacket.

Marissa started to tremble and shake. She had to get out of this room. As she pushed herself away from the chair she stumbled and tripped. But strong arms were there to stop her from falling, to hold her tight.

'Marissa, what happened? Are you okay?' *Oliver.*

\* \* \*

Oliver had thought Marissa was about to faint and hurt herself on the way down. Thank heaven he had come into the room, looking for her, when he did. As he held her tight in the circle of his arms, he felt a powerful urge to protect and comfort her. In this moment, she seemed so vulnerable, she who presented as formidably efficient and self-contained. She clung to him not just, he thought, for physical balance, but also for emotional support. What had happened here?

'Let it out,' he said. 'If you need to cry, do so.'

'I'm not crying,' she said, her voice muffled against his shoulder. 'I'm really not.'

He held her in silence, aware of her softness, her rose-and-vanilla scent, how much he liked having her there so close to him. He resisted the urge to drop a kiss on the top of her head. That would be too intimate, too personal, for a woman who had set very clear boundaries.

Finally, her breathing became more even. Marissa pulled away and looked up at him. She was very pale, in spite of the warmth of the room. There was no evidence of tears, but her make-up was smudged around her eyes and, without thinking, he reached down to tenderly wipe away the mascara smear with his finger.

'Thank you,' she said. 'And…and I'm sorry.'

He frowned. 'Sorry? Sorry for what?'

'For having you see my panic attack.'

'Panic attack? Is that what was happening? There's no need to apologise. I thought you were going to faint and fall, possibly get injured. I'm so glad I came into the room at the right time.'

'Thank you,' she said. Those unshed tears made her eyes seem even bluer. 'I'm glad you were here, too.'

'Are you feeling okay now?' he said, reluctant to step back from her. They were still close. At the same time, he was wary of treading where she didn't want him to be. 'Did you get bad news?'

'Not really. Not…not new bad news. It… it's the smell of the Christmas tree. The pine needles. They bother me.'

'An allergy?'

'In a way.'

'It's stuffy in here and the smell of the pine needles is very strong. We could open a window, but it would quickly get icy cold. It's bitter out there. They're predicting snow for Christmas. Besides, you wouldn't want wind coming through the window when you're decorating a tree in here.'

'It's not me dressing the tree, it's Andy.'

'So why are you in here by yourself?'

'Long story. But Andy asked me to keep the room free of guests and to keep an eye on these fragile, valuable decorations. I can't leave here until he gets back.'

'Why don't I ask Priya to send someone in here to take over guard duty, while I take you off for a cool drink or a coffee?'

'I don't want anyone to see me like this,' she said shakily.

'Let me take you to my apartment, where you can have all the privacy you want. If you feel like telling me why the scent of pine needles bothers you so much, you can. If not, you can take some time to get yourself back together and get on with your day.'

Her shoulders went back, and she stiffened. 'Are you worried this…this incident might affect the quality of my work? I assure you it won't. I'm on call twenty-four hours while I'm here.'

'I know how committed you are. I'm certainly not concerned about that. But I am worried about you.'

'Like a good fake boyfriend should,' she said

with a curve of her lips that wasn't quite a smile, her dimple the merest indentation.

'I wouldn't be much of a fake boyfriend if I didn't look after you, would I? But just as one human being to another, you're distressed and in need of a break and perhaps something to eat.'

'Ugh, I couldn't eat a thing,' she said, shaking her head. 'But I like the idea of going somewhere out of sight. And, to be honest, I'm curious to see the private areas of the building. I feel I owe you an explanation for why I collapsed all over you. And I'm very grateful to you for catching me.'

Within minutes of Oliver's calling Priya, she was there. Priya looked curiously at the somewhat dishevelled Marissa but, being a perfectly trained hotel manager, she didn't say anything except to reassure them that the room would be guarded until Andy returned with a new team of decorators.

Oliver kept his arm around her as he escorted Marissa to the private wing of the Manor at the east end. His grandmother still lived in the large house-sized residence fitted out for her and Grandpa when they'd converted their country house into a hotel. They'd sold off the farmland that had still been part of the estate to fund the conversion. As a child, he had lived there with them on his frequent extended visits, then permanently when his mother had left the country. When he'd turned twenty-one, his grandparents had given him his own spacious apartment in their private wing. They'd been so good to him. Paid for the law degree studies he'd dropped out of, as he'd found hotels to be so much more interesting. Helped bankroll the startup of his business. He could never repay them for what they'd done for him. Everything he'd ever been able to do for them had been worth it. Even pretending that Marissa was his girlfriend.

He showed Marissa to the oversized, squashy sofa—big enough for a tall man to stretch out on. Marissa sat tentatively on the edge, obviously ill at ease.

'Granny will be delighted I've dragged you to my lair so we can be on our own,' he said, sitting down next to her.

'Do you really believe Edith thinks that?'

'Of course she does. She'll be disappointed when you return to Room eight.'

'Which I now can't help thinking of as the Bogbean Room.' He was pleased to see her tentative smile—more of the dimple this time.

'Don't let Granny hear you say that. She would be horrified.'

'You think so?'

'I know so.'

Marissa looked around her. 'Your apartment is amazing. I could fit three of my apartment into it. Impeccably created by Edith, I suppose?'

'I was twenty-one when I moved in. I had no say in how it looked. Granny kept in mind what she thought I'd like when she chose the furnishing and decoration. It was done in a simpler style than the rest of the private wing, more contemporary but still with a nod to the building's ancient bones. Fortunately, it turned out she was right. In fact, I incorporated some of her design ideas into my penthouse at Pierce Soho they suited me so well.'

'What if you hadn't liked what she did here?'

'I wouldn't have told her. No way would I have wanted to hurt her feelings.'

'You would have pretended to like it?'

'Yes.'

She paused for a beat. 'You're good at pretending.'

'So are you. We wouldn't be getting away with the fake-relationship thing if we weren't equally good at pretending.'

'True,' she said.

But he wasn't pretending about how attractive he found her, how compelling. He couldn't remember feeling like this about a woman, certainly not over the space of a few days. It surprised him.

'Coffee? Or something stronger?' he asked, getting up from the sofa.

'A big glass of water, please.'

As Oliver poured the water in the kitchen, he remembered their discussion on favourite foods. He took a block of dark Belgian chocolate from the pantry, broke it into pieces and presented it to her on a plate. 'This might also help,' he added.

'How can I resist a man who gives me chocolate?' she said, but her voice was still shaky, and her smile didn't light her eyes.

'You did tell me it was your favourite food,' he said.

Oliver watched as she nibbled on the chocolate. She savoured every bite with exaggerated pleasure. It made him wonder if there was anyone back in London to look after her when she needed a boost to low spirits. Not to look after her in a patriarchal male way; he suspected she'd run a mile from that. Not in a warm, family way, either, as he knew her parents were dead and so was her godmother. But in the way of someone who cared about her and had her best interests at heart. Someone to be her wingman—or wingwoman. Perhaps that was Caity, but her friend ran a thriving business and would soon be mothering twins. Not that it was likely Marissa would ask for her friend's help. He got the impression she was so fiercely independent, she would tell him she didn't need anyone to look after her, thank you very much. Not a commitment-phobe like him, that was for sure.

But as he thought about Marissa, he realised he didn't have anyone, either. He had staff at his beck and call at his own hotels and here at Longfield Manor. Call room service from his penthouse and anything he wanted would be delivered within minutes. And his grandmother jumped at any opportunity to dote on him. He still saw his schoolfriend Toby on occasion, but Toby was married with young children and his family was his focus. Marissa had an air of aloofness about her that might very well be, he thought, loneliness. Was he lonely? He was surrounded by people and his business took up every second of every day. He didn't have time to be lonely.

Marissa downed the water as if she hadn't drunk for a week, then put her glass down on the coffee table. 'Do you mind if I sit back on your sofa?' she said. 'It seems too perfect to use with all those cushions so precisely arranged. I don't dare disturb them.'

'Toss the cushions on the floor if you want to. I do. But, again, don't tell Granny. She's a cushion fanatic. Wait until you see my bedroom. There are a million cushions on the bed.'

*What had he said?*

An awkward silence hung between them at the impact of his words. Inwardly, he cursed himself. 'I didn't mean—'

'I don't think—'

'You're not interested in seeing my bedroom? Point taken. But I won't pretend I don't want to see you in my bedroom.' He paused. 'In my bed.'

She flushed high on her cheekbones. 'And I won't pretend that I wouldn't like to be there. In your bed.' She met his gaze directly. 'With you.'

His breath seemed to stop, and his heart hammered at the sensual thoughts she conjured. Knowing she could match him made him want her even more.

She shifted away from him on the sofa as she continued. 'But I don't do flings and you told me you don't have long relationships. I've decided I want commitment and everything that comes with that. What you might find boring. Security. Marriage. Even kids. Not now. Maybe not for a long time. But it's what I ultimately want. Whereas you're not interested in being tied down. We're looking for different things.'

'That's true,' he said, thinking how crass his words sounded being quoted back at him. Had he really said that to her? Yes, he had. Because he always made it clear to a woman that short-term was all he wanted and that he would pull the plug if awkward emotions developed or demands were made.

'Truth is, I want you, but I also like you,' she said. 'Having a fling with you would most likely not end well. And I don't want that. Besides, I don't want to jeopardise this good thing we're doing for Edith by making things awkward and uncomfortable between us. So can we not mention your bedroom again?'

Oliver nodded. He would be respectful and not try to argue. Even as at the same time he regretted the lost opportunity to see where that mutual attraction might take them.

'And I'll take you at your word that there are lots of cushions in there,' she added.

# CHAPTER NINE

IN TRUTH, Marissa ached to count the cushions on Oliver's bed. To throw them one by one onto the floor followed by every stitch of Oliver's clothing—and then her own.

What had Caity said about Oliver? *Movie-star handsome.*

With his black hair and green eyes he was that all right—but he was so much more than his good looks. She was drawn to him like she'd never been drawn to a man—except, that is, his sixteen-year-old self. Who could have predicted that arrogant boy would grow up to be so thoughtful? But she'd meant every word about keeping her distance from him.

She was so attracted to this man it would be easy to let her senses take over. To share glorious sex—and she was convinced it would be glorious—with him with no thought of to-morrow. And then where would she be? Exactly what she would appear to be at the end of this seven days—another discarded girlfriend. Only she wouldn't have been a real girlfriend, rather a pretend girlfriend with benefits.

*Aargh!* She felt her head was spinning, not from the pine needles but by the realisation that she could fall for Oliver in a big way. Actually fall in love with him—and that would be disastrous. All those danger signs that had been beeping at her from the moment she'd realised who he was and what he'd been to her as a teenager were now urgently flashing a warning.

*Protect your heart.*

He was keeping a respectable distance from her on the sofa. How ironic. If there was anyone there to see them, they would have to keep up the pretence of their fake relationship and he would quite probably have his arm around her. But when there was no one there, they could be what they really were to each other— he the boss, she the contract employee. A possibility of something else he could be crept into her mind—*a friend.* They were halfway there; she enjoyed his company so much. If they kept out of that bed with its multiple cushions, could she and Oliver end up friends? Before the thought had a chance to lodge in her brain she dismissed it. For her, it would have to be all or nothing with Oliver. Because of the reasons she'd give him, *all* was never going to happen. Just these remaining five days.

'Thank you for the chocolate, for looking after me,' she said. 'I feel so much better now. In fact, I feel a little foolish. I probably would have been fine without—'

'Me catching you when you fell? I don't think so.'

He moved closer to her on the sofa. She was acutely aware of his warmth, his strength, the spicy scent of him, how grateful she was that he was there.

'You'd had a shock of some kind. Are you ready to tell me about it?'

Marissa angled her knees so it was easier to face him and took a deep, steadying breath. His expression invited confidence; his eyes were kind and non-judgemental. No matter, she still hated sharing her story—it never got easier. 'You deserve an explanation,' she said. 'You were right about it being linked to why I don't like Christmas. Why I'm reputed to be a Scrooge and a Grinch.'

He frowned. 'Surely not? Do people really call you that?'

'Sadly, yes. And it's true. Though only a very few people know why.'

She gripped her hands tightly together in front of her and looked ahead, rather than at Oliver. She couldn't, after all, face the pity she knew she would see in his eyes. He had a stark, black modern clock on the wall opposite that suited the room perfectly as its metallic hand ticked relentlessly around the clock face. She was shocked to note the time—there was so much to be done—but this needed to be said.

'Christmas used to be a big deal in our family. There were just my parents and me, my brother Kevin and my grandmother. Nana used to join us for Christmas, too. But my parents being the warm, hospitable people they were, our house was also open to waifs and strays who didn't have family to go to or were away from home. The house would be decorated to the max, and my parents cooked for days to have the full-on traditional feast with all the trimmings. If you'd asked me then, you would have heard me say I adored Christmas.'

She turned back to look at Oliver. Noticed that he swallowed hard. She'd told him her parents had died, but not how they'd died. He must have guessed she was about to recount something awful. She forced herself to continue. It was always difficult for her to tell someone what had happened. 'Five years ago on Christmas Eve, my mother and father were returning home with the Christmas tree when they were killed in a car crash. My mother went instantly, my father died later in hospital, early on Christmas Day.'

Oliver gasped. He moved closer, reached out, untwisted her hands and enfolded them in his much larger ones. 'I'm sorry, Marissa.'

She felt comforted by his touch, understood how difficult it was to utter more than platitudes at times like these. 'It was an accident, a horrible accident.' She would never, ever forget the shock, disbelief and deep, wrenching pain she'd felt when she'd been notified.

'The police couldn't be sure exactly what happened, as my parents were on a back road with no cameras. It was raining. The narrow road was slippery. They were running late with their decorating because of work commitments. Did they swerve to avoid an animal on the road? Did the tree slip free of its moorings and slide off the car? Perhaps they were rushing, driving too fast, but whatever the reason, the car went off the road and crashed head-on into a very solid fence.'

Oliver's grip on her hands tightened. 'I have no words. I can't imagine how you must have felt.'

'Because it happened at Christmastime, I can never forget it. Christmas is the anniversary of my parents' deaths. There were pine needles everywhere. All through the wreckage of the car, through...through my parents' clothes. My dad still had a few pine needles in his hair when he was in hospital. The smell... I hate it. It brings back so many bad memories. Back there, in the reading room, the scent was so strong I felt overwhelmed.'

'No wonder. There are pine Christmas trees everywhere you look at this time of year.'

'Which is why I try to avoid them. I wish more people used artificial trees, although nothing looks as good as a real pine. But even a fake tree symbolises everything I lost that Christmas.' She paused. 'You know, both Kevin and I had offered to pick up a tree for them, but Mum and Dad insisted it was something they liked to do themselves. They'd made collecting the tree a ritual since their first year of marriage.'

'So you and Kevin tormented yourselves with endless *if-onlys*. If only you'd gone instead... if only—'

'We tormented ourselves with many regrets and recriminations. As you can imagine, Christmas that year was hell. Organising funerals instead of festivities. The paperwork, the legalities, the pleasantries while accepting condolences, when all I wanted to do was crawl into a dark hole and howl.'

He squeezed her hand. 'My grandpa's death wasn't a tragic one like your parents'—'

'Every death is tragic when you lose someone you love.'

'But at least it was expected. Grandpa was eighty-seven with inoperable cancer. We knew we were going to lose him but that didn't make his loss any easier.' He paused. 'Granny was too distraught to handle the formalities, so I had to do it. Who knew how much time and effort was involved?'

'Every time I had to write down their details it was another blow, another reminder they were gone and I would never see them again. I was never that sure of the year of my father's birth when I was younger. I sure knew it after filling out all those forms. Then, just weeks after the accident, our grandmother died of a stroke brought on, the doctors said, by the shock of her daughter's death. My mother was her only child. As next of kin, I had to go through it all again for Nana.'

'Loss upon loss,' Oliver said hoarsely, his

grip tightening over her hands. 'How did you bear it?'

'We didn't cope well. When it was all over, we were left with nothing—no family except distant cousins in Norfolk we barely know, and friends who didn't know what to say so stayed away. My brother is two years younger than me. He took it very hard. The next year he couldn't deal with the prospect of Christmas without Mum and Dad. He took off on a trip to Australia and never came back.'

'What do you mean, *never came back*?'

'He met a wonderful girl, Danni, and they got married. He lives in Sydney permanently now.'

'That seems like a happy ending, though.'

'For them, not for me. It meant I lost my brother, too. I know that makes me sound selfish, and I don't mean it to. I'm really happy for them, and she's awesome. But they're just so far away.'

'Have you been to see them in Australia?'

She felt like she should get up and walk around the room, instead of sitting there, static. But she didn't want to lose the comfort of Oliver's hands cradling hers.

'The second Christmas after my parents' deaths, I flew down to Australia, glad to get away from London and the memories. Sydney is an amazing city. We celebrated Christmas with Danni's family. Although everyone was very kind and welcoming, I felt like an outsider, an interloper. As well, a traditional northern hemisphere Christmas celebration in a hot Australian summer just didn't seem right. And it wasn't different enough for me to forget my memories of that terrible Christmas.'

'I thought Aussies had barbecues on the beach for Christmas?'

'Some might. But I was told many prefer the traditional turkey, plum pudding, brandy custard, mince pies, Brussels sprouts, the lot. I felt so sorry for Danni and her family slaving away in a hot kitchen. I might not like Christmas but to me it means winter, fires roaring in the fireplace, frost and the possibility of snow. Like here, in this beautiful place. No wonder guests flock here at this time of year.'

'Sydney gave you another bad Christmas experience? I hope that was the end of it.'

'There's more to come. Are you sure you want to hear?'

'I do,' he said. 'I want to understand you, Marissa. I'm beginning to appreciate what an effort it must have been for you to come here as a Christmas event planner.'

'I did it for Caity. I'd do anything to help her.' She didn't go into detail; that was Caity's business.

'I see that now. I appreciate your help even more.'

'And I…well… I'm really glad I came.'
*And got the chance to meet you.*

'Dare I ask what happened the next Christmas?'

'The next year I decided to lock myself away in my flat for Christmas and come out when it was all over. Then out of the blue, I got fired from my job on Christmas Eve. The marketing company I worked for decided to close its event planning division. My position was made redundant.'

'That sounds grim. Can they do that on Christmas Eve?'

'It's heartless but legal, apparently. My Grinchiness really set in then.'

He slowly shook his head. 'A series of awful things that just happened to occur at Christmas. I mean, it's not really the fault of Christmas, is it? More like coincidence.'

'It's jinxed. Christmas is jinxed for me.'

'You can't seriously mean that.'

'Then how do you explain that the next year—last Christmas—I caught my boyfriend kissing another woman under the mistletoe at his office party. Passionate kissing. Complete with spiteful triumph from his so-called *just a friend* colleague.'

'Awful. Was the boyfriend a serious relationship?'

'I was gutted. I really liked him. He was a client and initially I knocked him back when he started asking me out. But he persevered. When he was no longer my client, I finally said yes. I fell hard for him. We were talking about moving in together.'

'That's serious.'

'As serious as I've ever got. And another regret. Up until then I had a strict *no dating a client* policy. That's been put in place again, I can assure you.' Not that anyone had tempted her with thoughts of breaking it again. Until now.

'Me being the exception,' he said with a smile.

'My policy didn't cover fake dating.' There it was, under all the angst, an easiness between them she felt very comfortable with.

He let go of her hands and got up. 'Would you like that coffee now?'

'Yes, please,' she said, also getting up to follow him to his kitchen, which was at the end of the open-plan living room.

'Where would you have spent Christmas if you hadn't come here?' he asked, as his impressive espresso machine steamed and hissed.

'I had flights booked to Nusa Lembongan, a small island off the east coast of Bali. Christmas isn't part of the culture there, so I figured I wouldn't be immersed in festive cheer like I would be in London. The tourist hotels cater for Christmas, but I don't think it would have been difficult for me to avoid any festivities.'

'Instead, you're here, working for me, immersed in our Christmas events.'

'And loving every minute of it.' She looked up at him. 'I mean that. Working here has been a revelation.'

'Except for incidents when you're confined to a stuffy room with a Christmas tree.'

'There's that,' she agreed. 'But look how chivalrously I was rescued.'

He laughed. 'And not just because I'm your fake boyfriend. Let's get that clear.'

She smiled. 'That's another problem with this job.'

'And what's that?'

'I can't include my stint as pretend girlfriend to the CEO on my résumé.'

'We might have to keep that one to ourselves.'

'I wholeheartedly agree,' she said. 'Also,

I'd appreciate it if you didn't share what I've just told you with anyone else. You know, my history regarding Christmas and why I'm a Christmas-phobe.' It was a relief to have told him, but she didn't want other people to hear her story, including his grandmother, Edith.

'That's understood. It's entirely your business. But thank you for opening up to me about the tragedy in your past. You've suffered quite the litany of grief, too much for one person. Tell me about your godmother. Did she pass at Christmas, too?'

'No, she died before my parents did. My mother took her loss badly. They'd been friends since primary school. And, before you ask, my cat didn't die at Christmas, either.'

'That's something,' he said cautiously.

She couldn't help but laugh at his comment, which lightened the atmosphere.

Oliver opened his pantry to pull out a packet of Italian almond biscotti. 'I keep stocked up on snacks. Needless to say, this kitchen isn't used much. Not when I live in a hotel.'

'Lucky you. I'd never use my kitchen if I could eat Jean Paul's food rather than cooking it myself.' What a difference her meal last night had been to her rotation of ready meals warmed up in the microwave, or hastily constructed salads.

'One night we could have dinner sent up here rather than eat in the restaurant,' he suggested.

'Do you think that's wise?' she asked, thinking how very unwise it would be for her to be alone with him—particularly near his bed or the inviting sofa.

'Probably not if you want to continue resisting my attempts to seduce you,' he said with a wry twist to his mouth.

Marissa's heart skipped a beat at the thought of a full-on seduction by Oliver, but she managed an appropriate response. 'Restaurant it is, then.'

She sat on a high stool at the kitchen counter to drink her coffee and he stood opposite her. 'Oliver, now that I've done so much soul baring, can you tell me some more about yourself? If it's not too painful, that is.'

He bridled and that easy moment of repartee evaporated immediately. 'Why would it be painful?' He shrugged. 'My parents weren't around a lot of the time, but I didn't lack for anything.'

She didn't reply, just let a silence fall between them, and waited for him to speak.

'Okay, except for parental love,' he said finally in a self-mocking tone.

Heartbreaking, she thought. 'A lack of love from your parents is kind of serious,' she said.

'Fact is, my parents weren't ready to have a kid. They hadn't known each other for long when my mother fell pregnant. I believe my father had doubts I was his, until I turned out looking very like him. A baby hardly fitted with their lifestyle—a model and a rock musician. They'd go away for months at a time and leave me with my grandparents. My schooling could only be described as erratic.'

She hadn't expected that, not when he came from wealth, his mother a well-known model and socialite—this place their ancestral home.

What was that old saying? *It's better to be born lucky than rich.*

'That doesn't sound great,' she said, not sure what else she could say. How grateful she was for her stable upbringing with parents who loved each other and their children, whereas Oliver seemed to have had terrible luck in that area.

'When I was eight, they put me in boarding school.' She knew he'd been in boarding school when he was sixteen but not as young as that.

He'd put down his coffee and she noticed his fists were tightly clenched by his sides.

'Eight? You were a baby. How was that?'

'By being sent away, I felt I was being punished, I didn't know what for. There was no actual abuse, but my years at boarding school didn't rate highly on the scale of my youthful experience,' he said.

The tight set of his jaw, the shadow that darkened his green eyes, told her not to probe any further. But she couldn't help shuddering. 'I can't imagine it would,' she said. She'd heard some traumatic stories about boys' private boarding schools; bullying, cruelty.

'The marriage was on and off with screaming fights then dramatic reconciliations. They finally divorced when I was thirteen. When I was fifteen my mother chased after a man to New Zealand and settled there.'

'She didn't take you with her?'

'I wasn't wanted,' he said baldly. 'Her excuse was that it was a bad time to interrupt my private schooling by moving to a different system.'

'I'm sorry, but that's out and out cruelty,' Marissa said fiercely.

'I suspect my mother lied about her age, and it didn't suit her to have people know she had a child my age. I was…inconvenient.'

'Of course you weren't inconvenient. Don't say that. It couldn't possibly be true.'

He sighed a weary sigh. 'Marissa, you weren't there.' His voice dripped with cynicism. 'All I can say is thank heaven for my wonderful grandparents.'

'No wonder you want to do everything you can to help Edith.'

'They were my real family. The reason I love Christmas at Longfield Manor was that my grandparents always made it special for me when I was a child, and even my self-centred parents made an effort to be here. Although one year neither of them showed up, without explanation. I waited all day for them.'

She wondered, as she had several times, about their conversation at dinner the night before. Oliver's confession that he had never been in love had surprised her. But if he hadn't received love from the people who were supposed to love him most, was he capable of giving love?

She slid off her stool and walked around to where he stood. 'You need a hug. For that sweet little boy. For that betrayed teenager. For the wonderful man you are now.'

She put her arms around him in a big hug. He hugged her back, powerful arms circling her. They stood there, close together for a long moment. Body to body. Arms wrapped around each other. He pulled back from the hug, their arms still around each other to look down into her face. 'Thank you,' he said.

'I'm sorry I made you dredge up uncomfortable memories,' she said.

'All in the past,' he said brusquely, with a *conversation over* stamp to his voice.

He looked down into her face, and she met his gaze unblinkingly. Her heart started to beat faster at his closeness. His face was already so familiar, those green eyes, his nose slightly crooked, his smooth olive skin, already at 11 a.m. darkly shadowed, his beautifully sculpted mouth. A mouth she knew felt so good against hers. A mouth she wanted to feel again for a dizzyingly pleasurable kiss. As she swayed towards him, her lips parted in anticipation. Nothing had ever felt better than being with this man.

Oliver's arms tightened around Marissa as he bent his head to kiss her. Her mouth yielded to his as she pressed herself close to him and kissed him back with passion and enthusiasm that matched his.

This wasn't pretend. It was as real as a kiss

could be. Her kiss was as exciting, as arousing, as their other kisses, but this also soared to a somehow different level. He knew it was because of the emotional connection he now felt for her. He understood her so much better after her confessions of heartbreak and loss. And she seemed to understand him, too. After revisiting his painful memories of abandonment, her spontaneous hug had been just what he'd needed but he would never be able to ask for. Somehow, she had known that.

*He didn't want to let her go.*

Yet, he would have to. He didn't have what it took to make a woman like Marissa happy. And her happiness now seemed somehow his concern. There should be no further kisses, no talk of seduction. She'd been honest about what she wanted for her future. He couldn't even commit to having a dog in his life, let alone a wife and a child. His focus was on a relentless drive to succeed. Riding the wave of the popularity of The Pierce Group hotels made him strive for more. He was looking for sites to expand into New York. Romantic relationships had never been part of his life plan.

One former girlfriend had accused him of being damaged. Not that she'd known of the tumultuous on-and-off relationship with his parents, particularly his mother. The way Mummy would arrive laden with presents, swoop down on him and cover him with kisses. Until boredom—with motherhood, with him?—had set in. Then she'd depart on a modelling shoot or on an extended holiday to heaven knew where, and he wouldn't know when he'd next see her. It was the same story with his father, although truth be told his father had never been effusive with affection. If it hadn't been for the love and stability given by his grandparents, maybe he would indeed be damaged. Although it was true that he didn't trust easily and was wary of commitment. And that sometimes he felt an emptiness that no amount of work and casual dating could make go away. But was that so uncommon in men of his age?

Marissa broke the kiss. Reluctantly, he let her go. She stepped back. 'I…er…have to get back to work,' she said, her voice not quite steady.

He looked down into her face. She was flushed and breathless and so beautiful his heart contracted. Not only was she the most gorgeous, sexy woman he'd ever had the privilege of kissing, she was also a thoroughly lovely person. Kind. Fun. Loyal. He really liked her. He'd only known her for two days, yet his gut

instinct was telling him—screaming at him—
that this woman was different from any other
woman he had met, that she could be special.
His gut instinct had never let him down. He'd
made good business decisions about people on
less acquaintance than two days, by listening
to it. Yet, this wasn't just about him, and the
last thing he wanted to do was hurt her.

'Are you sure you're feeling okay now?' he
asked.

'Quite sure,' she said. 'Again, thank you for
getting me out of that room and looking after
me. How did you know I was there?'

'Granny said you might be in the reading
room. I needed to talk to you.'

That wasn't strictly why he had sought
her out in the reading room. Truth was, he'd
missed her. He had simply wanted to see her
and reassure himself that this amazing woman
was still there under the same roof as him.
He'd spent a restless night thinking about her.
Wondering why he'd become so obsessed with
her so quickly. She'd made her position clear
that she wanted something more from a man
than a fling with a short use-by date.

*But what if he wanted more than that with
her, too?*

'I was looking for you to tell you I have to go to London for a few days.'

'Oh,' she said. 'That's a shame.' Disappointment flashed in her eyes before she blinked hard to dispel it.

'Something urgent has come up that requires me to be at my hotel in person.'

He'd been putting the visit off, but the way things were developing between him and Marissa meant now might be a good time for him to get away to London for a bit. The way that kiss, still warm on his lips, had made him feel was disconcerting. He needed to think through this mad attraction, these unsettling feelings, away from her. He didn't want sexual attraction to be mistaken for something deeper. He caught his breath. Was he really thinking about something deeper? He didn't like uncertainty. He needed to deal with this—and he could only do so away from the distraction of her beautiful face and body.

*Out of sight, out of mind.* Yet another useful cliché.

'I'll have to leave now,' he said.

'I understand,' she said. 'What will this mean for our fake relationship? How will I explain your absence to Edith?'

'She'll probably suggest I take you with me.'

'I couldn't do that,' she said hastily.

*Why not?* he immediately thought. But wasn't her not being with him what he wanted, so he could think things through without distraction?

'I'm needed here,' she said. 'I'm here to organise your Christmas and there are things to do, teams to coordinate.'

'Tell Granny that's why you can't go with me. She won't be surprised I have to go. A hotel is a twenty-four-hour business. After all her years here, she'll be aware that emergencies arise. And it's not always something a manager can sort, no matter how good they might be. There are so many variables, not the least of which is the people—including staff and guests.'

'I bet you have some interesting stories to tell,' she said.

The smile, that enchanting dimple, was back and suddenly he wished he wasn't going to London at all. This was confusing. And Oliver did not allow himself to get confused.

'There might be a few tales I could tell—with names blacked out of course.'

'I'll look forward to that,' she said. 'But... in the meantime, I...er... I'll miss you.' She was obviously having difficulty in meeting his gaze, her eyes cast down to her feet.

He tilted her chin back up with a finger, so he looked right into her eyes. 'Me, too. Miss you, I mean. It doesn't seem like we've only known each other for such a short time, does it?'

'Sometimes friendships work like that,' she said with a slow smile.

*Friendship?* Did she only see him as a friend? He wasn't sure he liked that idea. But surely she wouldn't kiss someone who was just a friend the way she'd just kissed him?

'Reassure Granny that we'll be in touch the entire time I'm away,' he said.

'I've got so much to do,' she said. 'We'll make Christmas super-special for you and Edith this year, I promise.'

'While you'll loathe every minute of it?'

'I won't lie and say I love Christmas, and now you know why. But it's so very different here from any other place I've experienced Christmas. I'll be okay. I can deal with it.'

'Will you be all right in the evenings?' Without him, he meant, but didn't like to say.

'Of course,' she said. 'Andy and I might go to the pub in the village for dinner tonight. It's been ages since we caught up.'

Jealousy sparked through him. Maybe it wasn't such a good idea to leave her. 'You're old friends?'

'We used to work together. I went to his wedding last year. It was such fun.'

'He's married?' he said, hoping the relief he felt didn't sound in his voice.

'His husband, Craig, is a wonderful guy. They're very happy. They travel the world together when Andy isn't working on Christmas trees.'

'That's good to hear,' he said.

'And I expect I'll have dinner with Edith tomorrow night. I think she'd like that,' she said. 'If I let her do most of the talking and am very careful with my responses, I should be okay.'

'Nice idea,' he said. He couldn't possibly be jealous of his grandmother enjoying Marissa's company for an evening, could he? He wasn't used to feeling this possessive about a woman. He wanted her with him.

*He didn't know how to deal with these unfamiliar feelings.*

'I think so,' she said. 'I really like Edith, despite her odd vehemence that you and I are a couple.'

'Right. Back to the fray, then,' he said, turning towards the door.

'Onwards and upwards,' she said. She looked sideways at him with a mischievous smile.

'You do realise everyone will think we sneaked up to your apartment for a quickie?'

He could only wish they had.

# CHAPTER TEN

Two NIGHTS OF Oliver being away from Long-field Manor turned to three, then four. Marissa missed him. She might pretend to herself that she didn't care—after all, how could she ache so badly for a man she'd known for such a short time? But she knew she was kidding herself.

*She cared.*

As he'd promised, although he seemed as flat out as she was, he kept in regular touch with brief businesslike texts and calls, even a video call. It was more contact than she might have normally expected between hotelier and contract event planner. And his cute emojis that accompanied the texts made her believe they were friends. Friends with the potential for more? Who knew?

When he returned in the morning of the day before Christmas Eve, she planned to be friendly but not over the top. Cool. Businesslike. A kiss on the cheek in greeting, as befit a pretend girlfriend who'd decided with him against public displays of affection.

That plan disintegrated the second she saw him. He'd asked her to meet him in the foyer of the hotel, near the recently placed, superbly decorated Christmas tree. She dressed carefully in a body-conscious deep purple knit dress and heels. She had her hair up in a messy bun and subtle make-up. She planned to be there before him and walked calmly down the staircase. Only to see him already there. Oliver. Tall and imposing in black trousers and cashmere sweater, and a very stylish charcoal-grey coat that spoke of Italian tailoring. He was talking to Priya behind the desk.

Movie-star handsome? *Oh, yes!* He was so handsome her heart accelerated into a flurry of excitement, her breath came short and she felt her cheeks flush.

For a moment she froze before she stepped down to the bottom step. Did he sense her closeness? He turned. For a very long moment they stared at each other across the distance of the foyer. Time seemed to stand still. There was just him and her and the ticking of the large antique clock. Then he smiled and she smiled back at what she saw in his expression.

She broke into a run towards him, to be swung up into his arms.

'I missed you,' she said, her voice breaking with a sudden swell of emotion, breathing in his heady, familiar scent. She almost didn't even notice the pungent smell of pine from the Christmas tree.

'I missed you,' he said at the same time.

'It's been awful without you,' she said. She'd counted every minute he'd been away.

'I cursed the problems that kept me in London longer than I wanted to be.'

'Video calls were not the same.'

'You can't hug a screen,' he said.

He kissed her, briefly but passionately. Oh, the joy of being back in his arms! She felt like she belonged there.

*How could something pretend seem so real?*

At the sound of clapping, Marissa broke away from Oliver's kiss to find Priya and one of the young admin staff smiling and applauding their reunion. All Marissa could do was smile back. It was impossible not to keep on smiling. Oliver was here.

'Thank you,' said Oliver with a slight bow and a grin to the hotel staff.

'We'll take this to my office,' he said to her.

'You can fill me in with what's been happening with the Christmas plans.'

He kept his arm around her, holding her close to him, as they walked the short distance to his office. Again, she had that feeling that she belonged there with him. That no other man would ever do.

Once they were inside the room, he closed the door behind them. Marissa looked up to him. It killed her to say the words, but they had to be said. 'You did that very well. The fake-girlfriend greeting, I mean.'

His face clouded over and he frowned. 'You think I was faking it?'

'I…assumed you were. That…that was our dating deal.' It was difficult to find the right tone. She hadn't realised just how badly she'd missed him until she'd seen him again, so familiar but still very much a stranger. Yet, he'd given her no indication that he felt anywhere near the same.

He put his hands on her shoulders. 'Marissa, not a word of what I said was fake. I genuinely missed you. In fact, I couldn't stop thinking about you and resented the time I spent away from you. Usually business occupies my every thought when I'm in London. Not so this time. Thoughts of you kept intruding.'

'Really?' she said, happiness and relief flooding her.

'What about you?' he said. 'Fake or real?'

She didn't have to think about her answer. 'Real all the way.' Her gaze took in every detail of his handsome, handsome face. 'I missed you and thought about you all the time.'

'Good,' he said, pulling her closer for a brief kiss before releasing her.

'I mustn't have done a good job of hiding how I was feeling, because I was constantly teased by Andy that I was pining for you, my boyfriend, the boss.'

'In reality, Granny is the boss.'

'Everyone here thinks of you as the boss, the new boss. They like and respect you. And some of them fear for the future of Longfield Manor. They're worried about Cecil retiring soon.' She paused a beat. 'Of course you probably know that.'

'Yes. He's worked for the family since my grandparents started the hotel. He'll be sorely missed and difficult to replace. Granny relies on Cecil so much and I'm worried about how she's going to take the news.'

Marissa laughed, but it came out as a kind of snort. 'You still think Edith doesn't know? Of course she knows Cecil is retiring. I sometimes wonder if you underestimate your granny, with her business acumen and people skills. Cecil and his wife are moving to Portugal. As he won't be on hand to advise his replacement, your grandmother is hoping you'll be here to keep your hand on the wheel as the hotel transitions to a new era, but she knows your Pierce Group hotels are your passion. I think she worries about the future of the hotel as she gets older.'

He nodded. 'You kept your ears to the ground while I was away.'

'Who else would the staff confide in than the boss's girlfriend?'

'And the fact that they all like you.'

'Perhaps. I like them, that's for sure.'

'They sing your praises. Anyone I spoke to while I was in London mentioned what a good job you were doing.'

'That's gratifying to hear,' she said. 'I don't know what you intend Longfield Manor's future to be. But you don't have to look far for someone to step into Cecil's shoes. Priya is excellent. A real gem. She knows everything about this place, how it ticks, peoples' strengths and weaknesses. She has some interesting thoughts about how certain things that have been done one way forever, could be done another, better way. She knows how to graciously interact with your grandmother, too.'

Oliver slowly nodded. 'I like Priya. I'll have to get to know her better. Perhaps put her through an interview process.'

'She'd be more than willing. And Cecil would approve of her taking over from him. I think he's been pretty much training her for the role.'

'I learn so much about what's been happening in my own home in my absence,' he said, but he smiled, and his words were in no way a reprimand.

'My priority is Christmas, of course, but it's been interesting to learn more about Longfield Manor.' She dreaded the prospect of saying goodbye to the hotel—and to Oliver—on Christmas Day evening.

'Back to our game of pretend,' he said. 'I was most certainly not pretending. My reactions were very real. In fact, when I saw you on the staircase, your hand on the railing, in that dress, not only did I think you looked hot, I thought you looked like you belonged there.'

'At Longfield Manor? I have come to love the place. Are you thinking of offering me a job?'

'Not at all. But come to think of it...'

She turned her head away, unable to meet

his gaze. 'I don't want a job here. I... I would find it hard to work with you, after our charade ends.'

Not when she ached to be his girlfriend for real. Anything else would be untenable. Imagine having to smile and be pleasant when he brought other women here, maybe even a wife. The thought of him with someone else was like the sharpest of stilettos stabbing into her heart.

However, practically, she could see a real role for her here, taking over some of the duties that had always been Edith's but were obviously becoming too much for her. A job as an in-house event planner. The hotel already hosted weddings and other functions but she could see further scope to capitalise on the location. A paid role for something Edith had always done for love and pride in her hotel. Such a job could be an answer to Marissa's dissatisfaction with her current freelance career. But it couldn't be. Not when she was on the edge of falling in love with the boss.

'Which brings us back to where we started,' he said. 'The line between real and pretend has totally blurred for me.'

Marissa stared at him, stunned speechless. 'Me...me, too,' she said breathlessly. 'I can no longer think about you in a pretend kind of way.'

He cradled her face in his hands and looked down into her face. 'I really like you, Marissa. I can't believe we've known each other for such a short time.'

'I… I really like you, too. So much.'

'I missed you so badly yesterday I nearly got in the car and headed down here to Dorset, leaving my business unfinished.'

'A trip to London to knock on your door entered my mind after the first two nights without you. Only…only I wasn't sure I'd be welcome and—'

He stopped her words with a swift, hard kiss. His voice when he spoke was hoarse. 'Can you, will you, stop looking at your role as pretend girlfriend as something irksome and—?'

'I never saw it as irksome.' It had started as fun, a game, a distraction from the reality of impending Christmas. A quiet poke back at that mean sixteen-year-old boy whom she now rarely gave a thought to.

'What I mean is could you see yourself transitioning into the role for real?' he said. 'As in…a real relationship?'

'To actually date you? To…to be your girlfriend?' She held her breath for his answer.

'Yes,' he said. 'That's exactly what I mean. What I want.'

This was so much more than she'd hoped for in those long nights he'd been away, and she'd realised how much she'd grown to care for him.

She let out her breath on a sigh. 'I would like that,' she said, a tremble in her voice.

He took her in his arms for a long, deep kiss, a kiss of affirmation of those unbelievable words.

*She was Oliver Pierce's girlfriend.*

'That felt more like a proper girlfriend kiss,' she murmured against his mouth, her entire body tingling with pleasure.

'I'm sorry, I should warn you that I can't promise you anything. I'm not good at making relationships last.'

'When you think about it, neither am I,' she said. 'Perhaps we should just take it day by day.' She couldn't worry about how long this thing with Oliver might last, if there was any future to it. She just wanted to be with him. Here. Now.

'I've never felt this way before,' he said, sounding bemused. 'So sudden. So quick.'

'Me neither. Your grandmother calls it a *coup de foudre*.'

His brow furrowed. 'A bolt of lightning?'

'Sudden, fast, powerful, from out of nowhere.'

*Love at first sight.*

That was what Edith said the French phrase meant. But Marissa wasn't going to share that particular translation with Oliver. Moving from fake to real girlfriend was enough for her to absorb, without progressing to contemplating actual *love*.

'That works,' he said.

'She said it was like that for her and Charles. That the power of that initial attraction kept their marriage strong through all those years—especially when things got tough.'

Oliver smiled. 'Grandpa used to look at her like he still couldn't believe she was his.' He paused. 'How come you were talking to Granny about *coup de foudre*?'

'She wanted to talk about us, of course. I had to tread carefully with her, as you know, so I didn't trip myself up. But I told her we liked each other straight away when we met.'

'Which was true.'

'It was, wasn't it?' She'd fought it because of a brief shared past he didn't even remember, but the attraction was too powerful.

He drew her to him for another, deeper kiss.

She wound her arms around his neck to pull him closer as she kissed him back. There was a substantial vintage leather Chesterfield sofa in front of the fireplace. She started to edge him towards it.

As she neared her goal, she heard a sharp knock then the door open. She stilled. Oliver had told her his granny never waited to be invited in, a leftover from when this had been his grandfather's study. Oliver pulled away from the kiss.

'Good morning, you two.' Edith practically trilled the words. By now, Marissa knew just how very much Edith wanted her grandson to be happy in a committed relationship.

'So glad you're back, grandson of mine. You were missed. Your lovely girlfriend missed you the most. She was moping around the place, quite lovesick, wishing you were here.'

'Edith!' said Marissa, laughing. She was getting quite used to Oliver's grandmother's outrageous assumptions and exaggerations. And yet…had the older woman been on to something, seen a spark of real attraction between her grandson and the event planner?

Oliver smiled. 'I missed Marissa, too.' He looked down at her. 'I've got used to having her nearby.'

Edith nodded approvingly. 'It was true Marissa did do some moping, but she was very, very busy, too. I've never seen the Christmas preparations carried out so efficiently. The decorations are superb. The heirloom accessories have been used in different ways and the new ones are stunning. And I think you'll really like the creative new ideas for the Christmas table settings.'

'We're ahead of schedule,' Marissa said. 'All the trees are up, and Andy will put the final touches on them today. Edith tells me that Christmas Eve is a big day and, as that's tomorrow, everything is on track for Christmas to start at Longfield Manor.'

'The trees look the best they've ever looked, thanks to your charming friend Andy,' said Edith. 'What a find he is. I've already booked him for next year's Christmas trees.'

'Smart move,' said Marissa. 'He gets booked up very quickly.'

'As it's Andy's last day with us, I've invited him to have dinner with me tonight,' Edith said. 'It would be great fun if you could both join us.'

Marissa looked up at Oliver. They shared raised eyebrows and a glance that told her he was looking forward to having dinner with just the two of them. But that it would be churlish not to accept Edith's invitation.

'Thank you, Granny, we'd like that,' Oliver said.

Marissa was disappointed not to be with Oliver, just the two of them, in his apartment for dinner. But she knew she would enjoy the meal with Edith and Andy and be able to relax now she and Oliver were officially dating. There'd be no need to be on edge guarding against slip-ups in a fake-relationship performance in front of her perceptive friend Andy—not to mention Edith's eagle eye.

Marissa had enjoyed her dinner alone with Edith on the second night Oliver had been away. Back on that night, she hadn't intended to pry into Oliver's past, but everything about him had become intensely interesting to her and she couldn't resist encouraging Edith's reminiscences. Edith had been only too happy to talk about her beloved grandson. She had told Marissa that, while she would never stop loving the daughter she rarely saw, she would also never forgive her for neglecting her child the way she had neglected Oliver.

'Little Olly was the dearest, brightest, most energetic little boy,' she'd said. 'We adored him, but grandparents can't fully make up for absent parents. Our daughter disappointed him so many times. Now he has no interest in her whatsoever, and I don't blame him—it's self-protection. He's done so well with his hotels and has big plans for expansion. But my husband and I were always concerned about the barriers he put up against letting people get close to him. Emotional barriers, that is. He always puts work before relationships. I mean, look at him now. He's up in London and you're here. That isn't right, especially just before Christmas.'

Marissa had reassured Edith that she totally understood why he'd had to go to London, because she was somewhat of a workaholic herself. Edith had seemed satisfied. Marissa's heart had swelled with compassion towards Oliver for what he had gone through as a child. All that wealth and yet he'd been starved of love from the people who should have loved him the most. But she had been left wondering if he would ever let her get closer.

She didn't see much of Oliver for the rest of the day, but Marissa didn't mind too much. It was like starting over with him, after the fake relationship had morphed into something genuine. Affectionate gestures that had been staged for maximum effect on an observer, now naturally sprung from genuine feeling and a desire to be together. The hunger for him was still there. But it was as if they'd given each other permission to take it slowly, to get to know each other better before they started tossing cushions off his bed.

Marissa felt energised by the shift in her relationship with Oliver. Reassured. *Happy*. There was still work to be done, the finishing touches put to the trees and decorations on this, the final day with the team of temporary staff. But they were nearing the finish line. As was customary, Edith hosted a lunch in one of the function rooms to thank the temporary crew for their work. Marissa was delighted to see that Edith's established people and the new crew recruited by Caity got on so well, working as a team. New friendships had been made. They hoped Edith and Oliver would have them back the next year. 'All in the spirit of Christmas,' Edith said.

Oliver disappeared for the afternoon with some of the crew, saying he had business in the village he needed to attend to. As he kissed Marissa goodbye, he said he'd see her at dinner. He didn't say what that business was, and she didn't ask him. She now knew him well enough to believe he was a man of his word. Still, she was intrigued. Curiously, Edith could not be drawn on his whereabouts.

That evening, as she made her way up the staircase to her room to get changed for dinner, she looked out the ancient mullion windows on the landing to the garden below. Andy had strung the large fir trees with the tiniest of twinkling lights. As she admired the spectacle, a lone deer made its way across the frost-rimed grass, stood in front of one of the sparkling firs and looked up at the building. For a long moment it was as if its gaze met Marissa's and she held her breath. At such a sight, even the most entrenched of Scrooges could not help feeling just a touch of Christmas magic.

# CHAPTER ELEVEN

LONGFIELD MANOR WAS completely booked out for the Christmas period and on Christmas Eve a high level of festive excitement thrummed through the high-ceilinged old rooms. It was that time of year when people didn't say hello to people they encountered, but rather, Merry Christmas. Oliver was kept busy with his grandmother greeting guests, many of whom were regulars returning for Christmas like they did every year. His grandfather's loss was felt, with guests offering condolences as well as greetings. Oliver was very aware that people saw him as stepping into his grandfather's shoes—but his grandfather's shoes didn't fit him, as Grandpa had known only too well.

The future of Longfield Manor was beginning to look very clear to him.

'Is all this making you too sad?' he quietly asked his grandmother. 'Are you sure you're okay with it? You don't have to greet everyone.'

'Absolutely I'm okay,' she said. 'Charles would expect it of me. Of course I miss him terribly. But you were wise to make changes to the way we celebrated Christmas this year. Things aren't quite the same, are they? Changes here and there, some more subtle than others? In a good way, I mean, an updated way, which shows we're moving forward. That makes it somehow easier to cope with. Thank heaven for Marissa.' She looked up at him. 'In many ways, thank heaven for Marissa.'

'I'll second that,' he said, not even trying to disguise the longing in his voice. 'She's wonderful in every way and I'm so grateful she's here with us.'

'She is special,' Granny said. 'And if I were you, I would think about getting a ring on her finger.'

'Granny,' he protested half-heartedly.

'Think about it,' Granny said. 'There is some magnificent heirloom jewellery in the safe, just waiting to be worn by a new generation.'

Oliver was getting used to having Marissa by his side. Where was she now? He was concerned that this immersive Christmas might be upsetting her, bringing back her painful memories of this time of year. Again, he marvelled at her loyalty to her friend Caity that had brought her down here, knowing she would be facing so much of what she hated and feared. He'd been calling her for the last half hour, but she must have her phone turned to silent. Had she locked herself away in her room?

'Granny, I've got to go find Marissa. Do you know where she is?'

'She's been flitting around checking everything she's organised is perfect for our guests. Right now, she's in the dining room with the head waiter, checking on the place settings with the new Christmas table linen. We're launching it tonight for the Christmas Eve carols dinner.'

'Thanks.' He turned to go.

'Wait,' said Edith. 'I said I'm okay. But I don't think I can deal with being Mrs Claus tomorrow.'

'I understand that might be difficult for you. Don't worry. I'll be Santa on my own.' He wasn't listening as hard as he should, keen to get back to Marissa. If he could, he would spend every minute of the day and night with her. Yet, he was taking it slow in their new, official relationship. They had time. He was thinking of taking her away somewhere after Christmas where they could be alone and private, away from interested observers.

'That won't work,' Granny said firmly. 'There must be a Mrs Claus. This tradition goes back a very long way, too long to break it.'

'I'll ask Priya if she can step in for you. Maybe next year you'll be feeling up to being Mrs Claus again.'

'Priya is a fine manager, but Mrs Claus has to be family. How do you feel about Marissa taking my place as Mrs Claus?'

He looked at Granny, aghast. 'Marissa isn't family, Granny.'

*Not yet, anyway.*

'Are you sure about that?' his grandmother said with narrowed, speculative eyes.

'I can't ask her to be Mrs Claus.'

He had honoured his promise to Marissa and not told anyone about her feelings about Christmas. So he couldn't tell Granny just why he couldn't ask this of Marissa. How it could traumatise her. She'd done enough for his family. Acting as Mrs Claus would be torture for a Christmas-phobe. And he didn't want anything to hurt or upset his lovely girlfriend. Not after what she'd been through. Not when she was beginning to mean so much to him.

'I couldn't ask that of her, Granny. And please don't *you* ask her. Promise me?'

He didn't quite trust Granny not to seek Ma-

rissa out and ask her herself. He had to find
Marissa first. He looked around. 'There are
Mr and Mrs Lee. They look like they want to
speak with you.'

He headed to the dining room to find Marissa heading out. How she could walk around
in those sky-high heels he didn't know, but he
liked the sexy sway they gave her. Her face lit
up as she saw him, and his heart turned over.
How had this woman become so special so
quickly? He kissed her in greeting. 'I've come
to find you before Granny does.'

Her brow furrowed. 'Why? Is there something she wants to ask me to do?'

'Yes. Well, I've told her not to ask you, but
you know what she can be like.'

'I'm intrigued. You'll have to tell me now.'

He led her away to a quiet end of the corridor. 'Granny has decided she can't face being
Mrs Claus this year. It would be too hard for
her without Grandpa as her Santa Claus.'

Her face softened. 'That's a pity. Poor Edith.
I can see it would be very difficult for her.
You told me they started being Santa and Mrs
Claus long ago when your mother was a baby.
Of course she wouldn't want to do it without
her soulmate.'

'That's right,' he said. 'It's just too sad.'

'Perhaps you should put the idea in moth-balls for this year?'

'Or I could play Santa Claus by myself.'

'Bachelor Santa,' she said. 'That could work.' She reached for his hands and pulled him towards her. 'Handsome Bachelor Santa.' She kissed him. 'You'll drive the lady guests crazy. Better steer clear of the mistletoe.'

He snorted. 'In the red Santa suit with a pillow down my front and a fake beard? I don't think so.'

'You could still be cute.'

'I could and I would. But Granny wants a Mrs Claus and she wants it to be you.'

Marissa dropped his hands and took a step back. *'What?'*

He put his hands out to placate her. 'I know. I told her I would not ask you. Of course I didn't tell her why.'

'To dress up as Mrs Claus and hand out presents, what torture that would be for a Scrooge like me?'

'You don't need to make light of it,' he said. 'I know Christmas holds painful memories for you and I totally understand.'

'And don't forget Christmas is jinxed, too.'

He wasn't so sure about that. 'It will have to

just be me as Bachelor Santa, whether Granny likes it or not. I'll tell her that.'

'Wait. Not so fast. Perhaps I... I should try it.' She bit down on her bottom lip. 'Being Mrs Claus, I mean.'

'You don't have to do that. Really.'

'I know I don't have to, but what if I want to? A Longfield Manor Christmas is somehow different. Quite out of my experience. It's like a different world. Also, despite my Christmas phobia, I've helped to create these celebrations.'

'You have. Everyone is delighted with the way things have turned out.'

She looked up at him. 'Maybe I need to face up to my fears. Being Mrs Claus wouldn't be desperately difficult. It's only for an hour or so, isn't it? Handing out gifts to the guests. Could it be any worse than helping to decorate a tree?'

'Perhaps not.'

'Does Mrs Claus go *ho-ho-ho*, too?'

'I don't think Granny ever did. It was Grandpa that liked to ham it up.'

'Was Edith a quiet, submissive type of Mrs Claus?'

'You could say that. She put talcum powder in her hair to be old Mrs Claus even when she was much younger.'

'So, a Mrs Claus with traditional values of what a wife should be? Defer to Santa?'

'I wouldn't like you to be like that,' he said. 'I want my Mrs Claus to be right up there with me sharing the spotlight.' Was he actually talking about Mrs Claus here or something altogether deeper? He just might be getting carried away.

'Equal rights for Mrs Claus?' she said.

'Something like that,' he said. 'But seriously, Marissa, you don't have to do it.'

'I know...'

'You really want to do it?'

She took a deep breath. 'Perhaps I need to challenge myself,' she said thoughtfully. 'Seeing everyone so happy and excited makes me remember what it was like before my parents died. What I'm missing out on. Do I want to run away from Christmas forever?'

'Only you can answer that,' he said. He hoped not. Christmas was important to him and he was beginning to hope that Marissa would be part of his life for Christmases to come.

Her brow furrowed. 'Only problem is the Christmas couple costumes. We brought them out of the attic to air. They're definitely old-style Claus family. Not to mention they wouldn't fit either of us. But it's Christmas Eve, there's no time to get new costumes or even alter the old ones.'

'Granny has thought of that, of course,' he said. 'Which makes me wonder for how long she's been planning the Mrs Claus switch.'

'I have long stopped wondering about your granny's motives,' she said. 'What do you mean?'

'She had a parcel delivered to me in London and asked me to bring it with me when I came back down here. When I asked, she said it was new Santa and Mrs Claus costumes. I put the box in the storeroom.'

'Let's go get it,' she said.

Marissa tore at the wrapping in her haste to get at the costumes. She pulled out the Santa one. 'Much nicer than the old one,' she said. She held the red outfit up against him. 'More streamlined, and the white beard is not so outrageous, either.' Her eyes narrowed and she pouted suggestively.

*Did she have any idea of what that did to him?*

'You'll look quite the sexy Santa in this.'

'If there weren't so many people around, I

might have to try it on and show you what a sexy Santa can do.'

To his surprise she blushed. 'I'd like that,' she said. She looked up at him, eyes wide and doing the dancing thing. 'Can I take a rain check on that?'

'There's a chimney in your room. Perhaps Sexy Santa can pay you a visit tonight?'

She laughed. 'I'll keep an eye on that chimney. Now, let's see what Mrs Santa's costume looks like.' She pulled a red garment out of the box and held it up. 'This is cute. I've said it before and I'll say it again, your granny has excellent taste.'

The outfit comprised a long-sleeved red velvet dress with a short, flared skater skirt, all trimmed with white fake fur. Marissa burrowed further in the box and pulled out red-and-white-striped tights, black ankle boots and a black belt with a big buckle that matched the belt for the Santa suit. Plus, the requisite Santa hat with a white pompom at the end that also matched Santa's.

'There are even Christmas earrings in the shape of reindeer.'

'I don't know about the earrings, but you'll look hot in that dress, Mrs Claus.' He waggled his eyebrows and attempted to leer.

'As hot as a woman could look in red-and-white-striped tights,' she said with a delightful little giggle. Had she giggled like that before? He wasn't sure, yet it seemed familiar and very much her.

'What makes me think this outfit was purchased by Granny with precisely Marissa Gracey in mind?' he said drily.

'Everything about it,' she said. 'And it's the right size, too.' She looked up at him. 'I can't not wear it, can I?' Delight and mischief shone in her eyes and it made him smile to see her like that. Again, he felt that urge to protect her and care for her, to want her life to be secure and happy after all the loss she had endured. Like his grandfather had cared for his grandmother. Maybe he was more old-fashioned than he considered himself to be.

'So you'll be my Mrs Claus?' he said.

'I will,' she said.

He helped her pack the outfits back into the box. 'I'll take the box up to my apartment to keep it safe. We'll make our appearances after Christmas lunch tomorrow.'

'It will be a big day tomorrow.'

'Are you sure you'll be okay about it all? No panic attacks?'

'I'll try very hard not to have a panic attack

but it's not something over which I have much control. But really, I'm determined not to let any jinx master ruin my time here with you in this truly wondrous place.'

'We're going to find ourselves without a second to spare tomorrow. Anything that's going to go wrong invariably goes wrong on Christmas Day. But after Boxing Day, things will settle down. There'll be more time for us to spend together then.'

She cleared her throat. 'You realise I'm meant to finish up tomorrow afternoon and head back up to London?'

Fear gripped him with icy claws. 'You wouldn't do that, would you?' He couldn't be without her.

'Not if you don't want me to.'

He put his hand on her arm. 'Marissa, I want you to stay.' If she went, he would follow her. Even if it meant leaving Longfield Manor in the middle of its busiest season.

'I'd like to stay here with you. I don't have any other work on, as I was meant to be on holiday in Indonesia.'

'Do you regret cancelling that trip and coming down to Dorset?'

'Not one bit. If I hadn't, I would never have met you. What a shame that would have been.' She paused. 'That didn't come out quite right, did it? I mean, we wouldn't have known we'd like each other if I hadn't agreed to the job and met you.' She smiled. 'Never mind, I think you know what I mean.'

'I know exactly what you mean,' he said, thinking how adorable she was.

There were so many things he badly wanted to say to her, but he'd never said them before and the words didn't come easily. It was too soon, anyway. After all he'd only known her for a week.

Marissa knew the Christmas Eve dinner at Longfield Manor was a very special occasion—the prelude to Christmas Day, which would be the pinnacle of Christmas excitement. For some of the European guests, Christmas Eve was the more important of the two days. The highlights of the evening were to be a special menu from Jean Paul and carols performed by the village choir. It comprised all ages and apparently was no ordinary choir—but a prize winner at national choral competitions. The choir was very much part of the community and led the door-to-door carolling in the village, too. That afternoon, Oliver had invited her to go to the village with him for the carolling, but she'd decided that might be a Christmas overload. Making a good show of being Mrs Claus the next day was more important.

Now she was at dinner with Edith and Oliver—back from the carols—at his private table in the dining room. She looked around her, quietly pleased at how fabulous the festive decorations looked, right down to the table settings. Thanks to Andy, the Longfield Christmas trees had become gasp-worthy in their splendour. People had got up from their tables to admire the dining room tree. Fortunately, it was set up some distance from Oliver's private table so she wasn't bothered by the scent.

The string quartet played background classical music as she, Oliver and Edith enjoyed the first two courses together. But then Oliver excused himself. 'I need to help out with the choir,' he said.

'If they need help, surely that's my job,' Marissa protested.

'You're off duty now,' he said. 'Stay and enjoy the music.'

Edith put her hand on Marissa's arm. 'Oliver has friends in the choir,' she said. 'You'll see.'

Marissa couldn't help but feel a little left out. Crazy really, when Oliver had done so much to make her part of Longfield Manor and Edith had made her so welcome. But everything between her and Oliver had happened so quickly, she still felt she was on shaky ground.

The string quartet started to play a medley of Christmas carols as the choir of twenty-five people trooped into the room, wearing the traditional chorister's white surplice over a red cassock and red Santa hats with a pompom on the end. The look was perfect for the occasion and the room. Marissa was stunned to see the last chorister to take his place was Oliver. He looked over to her and smiled, obviously aware she would be shocked. She smiled back, shaking her head in wonder.

'I had no idea Oliver was in the choir,' she whispered to Edith.

'He wanted to surprise you,' Edith whispered back. 'He used to sing with this choir and asked if he could join them again for tonight.'

'That's amazing. I never would have guessed,' Marissa whispered back. She couldn't keep her eyes off him.

The choir launched into 'The Twelve Days of Christmas' and continued with a medley of favourite carols.

Marissa realised straight away that the singers were superb—as indeed was Oliver, who sang in a deep baritone voice. When he sang solo in 'The First Noel' she was spellbound. She couldn't sing in tune herself, and deeply admired those who could. He was so talented and she was so proud of him.

'Wow…just wow,' she whispered to Edith.

She saw the same pride and love shining from his granny's eyes as she must see in hers.

She pulled herself up. *Love?*

Marissa could deny it to herself no longer. Of course she was in love with Oliver. But that didn't seem as disastrous a realisation as it might have been just a few days ago—because, with a secret fluttering thrill to her heart, she was beginning to sense he might be feeling the same way towards her.

That thought was confirmed when the choir moved to singing contemporary Christmas songs. As they started on 'All I Want For Christmas Is You,' Oliver broke away from the choir and danced towards her table. She caught her breath.

*The man could dance, too.*

He serenaded her with the song before lifting her out of her chair to swing her around in his arms. Laughing, she blushed bright red with embarrassment, enchanted by his gesture. His romantic move was met with clapping and applause and good-natured catcalls. When he dropped a quick kiss on her mouth the other diners cheered. After he guided her back to the table, she dropped back into her seat feeling bemused, elated and very happy. She had never met a man like Oliver Pierce—and she wanted him so much it hurt.

He had introduced her to a Christmas like she had never before experienced. She realised that listening to the Christmas carols hadn't left her feeling nauseated or panic stricken. When the choir sang 'Silent Night' she thought about her mother, who had loved that carol and although her eyes pricked with tears, all she felt was peace.

'When did Oliver start singing with a choir?' she asked Edith, keeping her voice low.

'When he was a young child living here with us, he sang in the church choir. Then he sang in choirs at his boarding school—I think it made the place more bearable for him. His father is a musician. He obviously inherited his musicality and voice from him.'

When the choir finished, to rapturous applause, Oliver joined Marissa and his grandmother at the table. She stood up to greet him.

'I can't believe you did that,' she said, smiling.

'You didn't like it?' he said with a grin.

'I loved it. You're a man of many surprises,'

she said. Marissa couldn't stop looking at him, wondering what other hidden talents he might have. She realised how little she really knew about him.

*She knew enough to allow herself to fall in love.*

'I don't want you to think I'm predictable,' he said.

'You were amazing. Such a talent. I'm in awe.'

'With that beautiful voice, he could have made a career of his singing, if he'd wanted to,' Edith said, ever the proud granny.

'I never wanted to make a career of it. No way would I ever follow in my father's footsteps. Singing for me is about relaxation and fun. So is playing my guitar.'

Oliver played guitar? He just got better and better. Not just movie-star good looks, but rock-star good looks, not to mention wealthy-tycoon good looks—and the talent and business savvy that took his appeal beyond his handsome face. She had a feeling that life would never get a chance to be boring around Oliver. And she longed to be part of his life. She realised with a painful jolt to her heart how empty her life would be if, her job here over, she went back to London and never saw him again.

'Is that where you went yesterday, when you disappeared?' she asked.

He nodded. 'Choir practice.'

'I'm glad you didn't tell me. Seeing you in the choir was a real surprise.'

'I was surprised at how much I enjoyed singing with them again. Unfortunately, my life in London doesn't allow time for a choir. So I'm making the most of being in this one. Part of the deal that the choir took me back was that I sang with them for the midnight church service in the village tonight. Would you like to come with me?'

One part of her wanted to go, another feared that might be too much Christmas overload. 'Thank you, but no. Mrs Claus needs her beauty sleep.'

'Mrs Claus is beautiful just the way she is.'

'But her looks are not enhanced by dark circles under her eyes.'

'I could debate that.' He paused. 'Do you have surprises in store for me?'

His question surprised her. She shrugged. 'Me? You'd roll around laughing if you heard me sing. What you see is what you get.'

'Sounds good to me,' he said.

'Can I tell you something?'

'Any time.'

She looked up at him, hoping he would understand that her words weren't spoken in jest. 'I can't sing it, but I can say it. All I want for Christmas is you. And I'm very glad you want me for Christmas, too.' When she kissed him, it was to gentle applause from the tables nearby.

# CHAPTER TWELVE

IT WAS CHRISTMAS MORNING, her clock had ticked over past midnight more than an hour ago, but Marissa was still restlessly awake in what she took delight in calling The Bogbean Room rather than the somewhat pedestrian Room eight. She'd looked up the Dorset wildflower to find it was a plant that grew in damp soil with clusters of white star-shaped flowers. Not such a bad name for a room after all. That was if the mundane name was accompanied by an image of the pretty flowers. On the door.

*Aaargh!* Why was she letting irrelevant thoughts like that churn around her mind and keep her awake?

Then there was the song the choir had sung that urged 'Santa baby' to hurry down the chimney. It was going relentlessly around and around in her head. Oliver had teased her by saying he was going to do just that.

*There's a chimney in your room. Perhaps Sexy Santa can pay you a visit tonight?*

Would he? Could he? *Did he really want to?*

A quiet knock sounded at her door. She smiled a slow, secret smile to herself as she got out of bed to answer it. Through the security peephole, she confirmed it was Oliver.

'You came by the door,' she said, pouting, pretending to be disappointed as she let him into the room and shut the door behind him.

'I didn't dare risk the chimney tonight. It's started to snow, so not such a good move to be clambering over an ancient, slippery roof in an effort to find the correct chimney.'

'Wise move,' she said. She wound her arms around his neck to pull him close. 'If you were covered in black chimney soot, I might not want to do this.' She pressed a kiss to the curve of his jaw, loving the roughness of his stubble against her skin.

'I don't think I'd care if you were covered in soot, I want you so much,' he said hoarsely, his hands around her waist.

'I want you, too, so much,' she said with a hitch to her voice. 'But if soot was a concern, I might have to strip off your clothes and take you into the shower with me.'

'Forget the soot, feel free to strip me anyway and drag me into the shower. If you strip, too, I'd go willingly.'

'I'd prefer it if you strip me first,' she said. 'And the bed might be more comfortable than the cold tiles of the shower cubicle.'

She reached up to claim his mouth in an urgent, hungry kiss that went on and on.

*The man could kiss.*

The time was way past for saying no to more than kisses. She wanted to make it clear she was saying yes to wherever he wanted to lead her.

She pressed her body against his, intoxicated by his now familiar scent, instantly aware of his desire for her and she shuddered with the answering desire that flooded her. She was wearing boxer shorts and a tank top. When he slid his hands up inside the top to caress her breasts, she gasped her arousal. 'Take it off,' she said. 'Now.'

'With pleasure,' he said hoarsely, sliding her top over her head and tossing it on the floor.

When his hand moved lower under the boxers, she moaned her pleasure and arousal. He knew just what to do to ignite her pleasure zones.

'My turn,' she said, pulling his cashmere sweater up over his head, followed by his T-shirt. That left him in only his black jeans. 'Oh my…' Marissa breathed, feeling light-headed as she feasted her eyes on his powerful chest, his six-pack.

She caressed his chest with the flat of her hands, revelling in the feel of smooth skin over hard muscle, the right amount of dark body hair. She fumbled with his belt, but her fingers were awkward with nerves and the more impatient she was, the less luck she had in undoing it.

'Let me,' he said. Soon, she was sliding his jeans down his thighs, her excitement levels soaring.

'Darn!' He was still wearing his boots and the jeans were going nowhere. He laughed. 'Again, let me,' he said, as he kicked off his boots and socks.

Then he was there in just his boxers. He kissed her again and she pressed herself close, warm bare skin against bare skin. There was a mirror behind him, and she looked up to see his back view reflected in it. Broad shoulders tapered down to the best butt a man could ever have. She almost swooned at the erotic vision of their nearly nude bodies entwined, her pale skin against his olive. She kept in shape, and clearly so did he, and she thought they looked beautiful together. It was another level of turn-on.

'Bed or bathroom?' he said.

'Bed,' she choked out. They could shower together some other time.

He picked her up and effortlessly carried her to the bed, an experience she found thrilling. He laid her on the mattress and lay down beside her, resting on his elbow as he looked down at her with those amazing green eyes. He traced her mouth with one finger. 'You are so beautiful.' His gaze roamed over her body and she felt it like a caress. 'Perfect, in fact.'

'I'm glad you think so,' she said huskily. 'You're utterly wonderful and perfect and I'm so very glad you're here, even if you didn't come via the chimney.'

'I couldn't have stayed away. I didn't want you to wake up alone on Christmas morning.' He paused. 'And I couldn't stop thinking about how much I wanted to make love to you.'

'What a magnificent man you are.'

'Says she, in the first flush of attraction,' he said, laughing.

*Not quite the first.*

She knew she should remind him of their first meeting but again, it didn't feel like the right time.

His hands slid below her waist and divested her of her boxer shorts. She did the same to him, taking time to explore and caress him while she did so.

He kissed his way down her bare skin to take her nipples in his mouth, one after the other, teasing them with his tongue until she ached for release. Then he explored her body with his hands and mouth until she bucked against him. 'Please, I want you inside me. Now.'

He took a condom from the thoughtfully provided amenity pack in the bedside drawer, and she helped him put it on. Then he entered her and she welcomed him into her body. He fell into just the right rhythm for her and she orgasmed before he did and then again after, melting in ecstasy. The man sure knew how to please her. 'I have to say again how wonderful you are,' she murmured sleepily. 'When I said all I wanted for Christmas was you, I knew what I was talking about.'

She fell asleep in his arms, feeling happier than she could remember feeling for a very long time.

They awoke early in the morning, to the sound of church bells pealing out a joyous Christmas message and made love again. This time their lovemaking was tender and unhurried, building to a powerful, mutual climax before they sank back into sleep.

Marissa woke later to find Oliver sleeping beside her, his arm slung across her. She admired him for a long minute, his face even more handsome in repose, his body strong and sleekly muscled. How lucky she was to have found him. She slid out from under his arm, so as not to disturb him. The room seemed oddly quiet, with no noises coming from outside, just the steady sound of his breathing from inside.

She shrugged on the ink-coloured velour hotel robe she'd left on the chair and padded barefoot over the lush carpet to the window. She drew back the heavy curtains. Snow. She watched, entranced, as a flurry of fluffy snowflakes drifted past the windowpanes. The gardens below had been transformed by a heavy coverage of snow. The lights Andy had strung up on the fir trees struggled valiantly to twinkle through the layer of white that now frosted their branches. She might have to get some help to shake some—but not all—of the snow off.

Oliver came up from behind her and slipped his arms around her. She leaned back against him, rejoicing in their closeness, the warmth and strength of his body clad in the matching robe to hers he'd taken from the closet.

'It's unbelievably beautiful, isn't it?' he said

softly. 'All the familiar landmarks transformed into something magical. Form becomes more important than colour or scent or anything else but this purity. A white Christmas. We'll have some very happy guests, especially those from Australia and South Africa.'

'It's utter magic,' she murmured. But the real magic was being here with Oliver, in the security of his arms around her, her body aching pleasantly from the sensual aftermath of intensely satisfying lovemaking.

'Thank you for letting me stay with you,' he said. 'As I said, I didn't want you to wake up alone on Christmas Day.'

'I'm so glad you stayed.'

'Now I don't know whether to wish you a Merry Christmas or not.'

'Please do. I think being here with you, becoming so involved with the Longfield Manor festivities have helped me. Perhaps, just perhaps, the jinx has been lifted. Maybe I can allow myself to enjoy Christmas this year without the fear that something terrible will happen.'

'I sincerely hope so. Do you think you'll ever be able to remember your parents without connecting their loss to Christmas?'

'I'm beginning to believe I will. Maybe one

Christmas I'll even be able to eat a mince pie again without breaking down. They were my dad's favourite, you see.'

'Grandpa loved them, too. Can't say I care for them myself. Jean Paul's fruit pastries are far superior in my opinion.'

'I'll try them and I'm sure I'll enjoy them.'

'Maybe that's what Christmas will mean to you this year. Laying down new memories. Not banishing the old ones, but letting happy new memories override them.'

'What a lovely idea,' she said, hoping fervently that it could be so, thinking how perceptive he was.

Oliver turned her to face him, searched her face. 'Perhaps some of those happy new memories could be made with me, Marissa?'

Her heart leapt. This was something she hadn't dared to let herself imagine. 'Perhaps…'

'I know we haven't known each other for long but, as I've said before, it seems like you're meant to be part of my life. Not just for Christmas but into the New Year, too, and beyond. Maybe next year we could be enjoying Christmas together again at Longfield Manor?'

Exultation at his words fought with caution. 'That's a beautiful thought.' Could she trust this man who'd made it so clear he didn't want commitment? How she wanted to believe in a future together. But it was a big step forward.

'You're thinking that's perhaps too great a leap?' he said, obviously sensing her doubt. 'Maybe we could go away by ourselves in the New Year to talk about how we could make our relationship work? Paris maybe? Or anywhere you would like.'

'Paris would be perfect.' She could think of nothing better. Just him and her.

He cradled her chin in his hands, in the way she had come to love. It made her feel cherished, special, safe. 'I really like you, Marissa,' he said. He could not seem more sincere.

'I like you a lot, too. Being here with you means so much. I... I would like to look into the future with you.'

'So, I can wish you Merry Christmas?'

This Christmas was so different. 'Please do. Although I'll wish you a Happy Christmas.'

'Is there a difference?'

'You wouldn't think so, would you? My father had this eccentric old aunt who used to spend Christmas with us. She was a sweetie, but she very primly used to say that *merry* meant drunken, and that to wish someone a Merry Christmas meant you were wishing them a Drunken Christmas and that was simply not on. You can imagine the fun my brother and I had with that one. We thought it hilarious and, for a while there in our lives, it was probably true.'

'But you say Happy Christmas now?'

'I just got to like happy better than merry. Happy is the best thing you could wish a person to be, isn't it?'

He laughed. 'I think it's kinda cute that you do.'

He let her go and headed over to pick up his jeans from where Marissa had tossed them the night before. She was disappointed that he was going to cover up his gorgeous body that had given her so much pleasure. But no. He didn't put on the jeans but rather dug into a pocket and pulled out a small, professionally wrapped parcel. 'Merry Christmas, Marissa,' he said, handing it to her.

'A gift for me? Really?'

'It's Christmas morning, Marissa. Gift-giving time.'

Of course it was.

She tore off the wrapping—she was never very good at decorously opening a present or reading the card first—to find a small box embossed with the name of a famous London jeweller. With trembling fingers, she opened it to find a bracelet of finely linked platinum studded with diamonds. She looked up at him. 'Oh, this is lovely,' she said. 'But it's too much, I—'

'I wanted to get you something special,' he said.

'This is special, all right,' she said. 'But—'

'Let me help you put it on,' he said. He fastened it to her right wrist. 'It fits perfectly. I bought it when I was in London and had to guess the size.'

She held up her hand to admire it. 'It's a lovely bracelet,' she said. 'But it's very extravagant of you.'

'You deserve something lovely,' he said. 'If this is prevarication because you don't like it—'

'No, I love it, I really do,' she said. 'It's just I wasn't expecting...' She kissed him on the cheek. 'Thank you very much. I shall treasure it.'

She went to the drawer under the desk and, in turn, pulled out a parcel of her own.

'Happy Christmas, Oliver,' she said, handing it to him.

'Me? You bought me a gift?'

'Why would you be surprised?' At the time she'd been unsure whether or not it would be appropriate, but she'd gone ahead anyway. She'd bought his gift from a shop in the village, and something for Edith, too, the afternoon she'd gone in with Andy. Then wrapped it in some exquisite paper she'd found in the same shop.

Would he like it? Oliver pulled out the soft, charcoal-grey Italian designer cashmere scarf in a muted windowpane check with an exclamation of pleasure. 'Thank you,' he said, holding it up. 'It's my favourite colour and perfect for this weather. How very thoughtful of you.'

'Are you sure? I wanted to buy you a book, but I felt I didn't know you well enough to know what you like to read.'

'The scarf is better. I confess, I don't get much time to read.'

'Let me,' she said, taking the scarf from him to put around his neck. She stood back to admire how it looked, somewhat incongruous in the neck of a hotel dressing gown. 'Yes, the colour is great on you.'

Truth be told, he would look good in any colour. Oliver dressed with a natural flair and style that befit a man of his position as CEO of London's most fashionable hotels, and heir to this awesome ancestral home.

But she liked him best wearing nothing at all.

# CHAPTER THIRTEEN

OLIVER HAD NEVER imagined the day would come when his grandparents wouldn't be playing Santa Claus and Mrs Claus on Christmas Day. The fond memories stretched right back to when he was a toddler.

And now he was Santa Claus and Marissa had stepped in as Mrs Claus. He wasn't sure Mrs Claus was meant to be so beautiful and sexy. Maybe Granny's interpretation of Santa's wife with a lacy white cap on grey hair pulled back into a bun, and wire-framed spectacles was more customary. But then he was only a thirty-two-year-old Santa, despite the white curly wig and ill-fitting beard. He wouldn't fool a kid that he was the real deal for a minute, that was for sure.

Marissa looked sensational in the new Mrs Claus outfit, her luxuriant dark hair waving from under her Santa hat to around her shoulders, her lipstick a rich, kissable red, the short skirt and striped tights showing off slender legs that went on forever. She'd replaced the plastic boots that came with the outfit with her own high-heeled black boots, which also added to the hot new Mrs Claus look. He didn't want her to take that outfit off after the gift-giving ceremony. He'd like to slowly strip it from her and make love to her. If he'd thought he'd been obsessed with Marissa before they'd spent the night together, it was nothing on how he felt about her now.

The Christmas feast was over. The guests who chose to take part in the gift-giving had gathered around the spectacular towering Christmas tree in the spacious guest living room. It was time for Santa and Mrs Claus to give out the presents, one for each adult guest. There were also age-appropriate gifts for the few children who accompanied their parents.

Christmas here was more an occasion for well-heeled adults than lots of kids tearing around the place. But Oliver liked their presence—Christmas didn't seem like Christmas without children. For the first time, he let himself imagine what it might be like to have *his* children spending Christmas at Longfield Manor. Little dark-haired children, because surely he and Marissa would have dark-haired babies—

*Stop!* He couldn't let his thoughts stray in that direction. Not now. Not yet. Maybe never, depending on what she thought of the idea.

This year the adult's gift was a handblown glass frosted bauble tree decoration with a resin miniature of the hotel inside it and the words *Longfield Manor* and the year hand-painted in silver script on the outside. It was an exquisite keepsake, the brainchild of Caity. He had a lot to thank Caity for—not the least of which was bringing Marissa into his home and his heart. Marissa reported her friend was doing very well in hospital, which pleased him.

Granny introduced the new Claus family, with a heartfelt homage to Grandpa, announced her retirement as Mrs Claus and then the ceremony commenced.

Who knew this could be so much fun?

Marissa was a brilliant sidekick and they traded banter and laughter with each other as they handed out gifts and well wishes to the guests. She was lovely with the children, squatting down to their level, giving hugs where appropriate. You would never guess Marissa was a Christmas-hating Scrooge. But might that be because she was that no longer? Thanks in part, he liked to think, to him?

When the gift-giving was over, one of the guests pointed out that Mr and Mrs Claus were standing right under a strategically placed bunch of mistletoe. Wasn't it time for Santa to give his wife her Christmas kiss? He looked to Marissa and she smiled back. Santa obliged with a passionate kiss and a backwards swoop of Mrs Claus. By now everyone knew they were a real-life couple.

'Are you two going to be naughty or nice tonight, Santa?' a longtime guest, who had known Oliver as a child, called out.

Marissa looked up at Oliver with wide eyes and a lascivious smile. Then she looked back to her audience and gave an exaggerated wink. 'Both naughty *and* nice,' she said in a slow and sexy voice.

To the guests' laughter and applause, Granny took the spotlight to thank everyone for choosing Longfield Manor to spend Christmas. She reminded them to book now if they planned to return next year, as returning guests had priority.

'I'll finish by thanking Marissa and Oliver for being such a brilliant Mr and Mrs Santa Claus.' She made a dramatic pause. 'And to express my opinion that they'd make a brilliant Mr and Mrs Pierce, too.'

'Granny,' groaned Oliver. 'That's going too far.'

But people were laughing and applauding, and Marissa didn't look embarrassed or upset; in fact, she was laughing, too.

And, really, was the Mr and Mrs Pierce thing completely out of the ballpark? He had never, ever felt for a woman what he felt for Marissa. He might need to think about securing her.

'Sorry about Granny,' he whispered to Marissa. 'She really got carried away this time.'

'Water off a duck's back,' she said. 'Nothing Edith says shocks me anymore. She means well. Remember, everything she says is motivated by love for you and her desire for you to be happy.'

Marissa was beautiful both inside and out. He hugged her, so grateful for the way she was unfailingly good to Granny. And the fact was, that since Marissa had been here, Granny had had very few forgetful or disoriented episodes. She was her old self more often than not.

The gift-giving over, waiters brought around trays with flutes of champagne and plates of exquisitely decorated festive cookies. 'These beat a mince pie, hands down,' Oliver said to Marissa.

She took a cookie shaped like a Christmas bell off the tray and nibbled. 'You're right. It's delicious. In fact, I might have to have another one. A Christmas stocking one.'

Oliver stepped away to call the waiter back with the tray, when Granny came over. She took his arm. 'Look who just got here. Such a lovely surprise. Toby and Annabel.'

Oliver was pleased to see his old friend. He greeted him with a hug. Then unhooked his Santa beard to better kiss his wife, Annabel, on the cheek—an awkward procedure with the Santa beard. 'Where are the kids?'

'Annabel's parents have a house down here so we're spending Christmas with them,' said Toby. 'They're minding the children to give us some grown-up time. You've always said I've got a standing invitation to visit, so here we are.'

'Great to see you. I must introduce you to my girlfriend.'

Toby's eyebrows rose. 'You? A girlfriend? One that lasts more than a week?'

Marissa had her back turned to them, chatting animatedly to a guest. Oliver tapped her on the shoulder and excused himself to the guest. 'May I borrow Mrs Claus? There's someone I really want her to meet.'

'Who?' Marissa said, turning to face him.

With a hand on her elbow, he guided her towards his friends.

'My old friend Toby,' he said. 'We go back a long time.'

He felt her stiffen. Perhaps it was too soon to be introducing her as his girlfriend.

'Toby and Annabel, let me introduce—'

'Marissa,' said Toby. 'So you two finally got together after all.'

The colour drained from Marissa's face.

*This couldn't be happening.*

Marissa was so shocked she couldn't speak, just looked from Toby to Oliver and back again. She barely registered Toby's blonde wife, who was looking curiously on.

'Do you remember me?' Toby said.

'Samantha's brother,' she said. 'How is she? We lost touch a long time ago.'

Toby wouldn't be diverted. 'Sam's fine. But how about you two? This is a surprise. Olly, you sly dog. I thought you didn't see Marissa again after that summer we first met her. So long ago. How old were we? Sixteen?'

Marissa could see recognition slowly dawn on Oliver's face. Recognition and a tight, contained anger. 'Yes,' he said, tight-lipped, not looking at Marissa.

'And you were fourteen, right, Marissa?' Toby said. He looked her up and down. 'You sure have changed.'

'One tends to in sixteen years,' Marissa said through gritted teeth.

'You wanted to ask her out then, didn't you, Olly? But Sam told us her parents wouldn't allow it. She was too young to date.'

'I don't remember that,' Marissa said, trying to force a smile.

'Nah. I reckon Samantha only said that because she fancied Olly for herself,' Toby said. 'She was right peed off that he only had eyes for sweet Marissa.'

*Sweet Marissa?*

How about Monobrow Marissa? Gawky and giggly? Now she remembered she hadn't liked Toby very much back then, though she'd been forced into his company in the school holidays. And after that overheard conversation, she'd completely avoided him.

'Sounds like something Samantha would do,' Annabel said, shooting a sympathetic glance to Marissa.

'So when did you and Marissa hook up again?'

*Hook up?* Was Toby being purposely offensive?

'Quite recently,' said Oliver, still not looking at Marissa. 'We met at a function at The Pierce Soho.'

'Did you recognise her straight away? Bet you didn't.' He ran his fingers across his eyebrows. 'The eyebrows, right?'

'I think you've said enough, Toby,' his wife interjected.

'She was just as lovely,' Oliver said, without actually answering Toby's question.

'I didn't recognise him,' Marissa said, not daring to look at him. 'He was Oliver Hughes then, if you remember. I had no idea he was the same person.'

*For a while, that is.*

It wasn't excuse enough for not reminding Oliver they'd met before, and Marissa knew it. She'd had several chances to tell him. Now she'd blown it.

She tried to change the subject by asking Annabel about the children, but their conversation was stilted.

'I'm sorry, it's been lovely to meet you, but I'm helping Edith with something, and have to go find her,' she said after one too many awkward silences. 'Catch up later?' she said, knowing full well she wouldn't.

'I look forward to seeing you again,' said Annabel.

'Me, too,' said Toby, homing in for a kiss that Marissa adroitly avoided. He reeked of alcohol.

'*Merry* Christmas,' she said.

'I'll be back,' Oliver said to his friends. 'Grab some champagne.'

He followed Marissa out of the room and into a deserted part of the corridor, not giving her a chance to gather her thoughts, let alone to plan any kind of strategy. A grim-faced Pierce male ancestor with mutton-chop whiskers from the Victorian era peered down at her from the wood-panelled wall.

His equally grim-faced descendent took her by the arm, forcing her to look up at him. 'Why did you lie to me?' he said, his eyes cold and accusing.

'I didn't actually lie. It was more of a…a… lie of omission.'

'A lie is a lie. I don't tolerate liars, Marissa. In any shape or form.'

'Understood,' she said. She wanted to say she didn't, either, but that might seem more than a tad hypocritical.

'Did you recognise me straight away?' he said.

'You looked like Oliver Hughes, but you were Oliver Pierce. I had no idea there was a connection when I agreed to work here. Oliver isn't an uncommon name.'

'A misconception easily cleared up, I should imagine.' He let go of her arm.

'Yes, the first morning I was here. All it took was an internet search.'

'Why didn't you remind me straight away that we'd met?'

'Because you had no idea who I was, and I decided to leave it that way. I was only going to be working here a week. I didn't know you were going to ask me to be your fake girlfriend.'

'And you still didn't tell me.' His eyes narrowed. 'You know, I thought there was something about you that was familiar, an expression, a giggle, but I meet so many people.'

'What you don't realise is that I loathed you.'

*'What?'*

'Back then, I actually had a huge crush on you. Huge. Then I overheard you talking to Toby. Shredding my appearance to pieces. There wasn't anything about me that you both didn't snigger and sneer over. I was gawky, flat-chested, giggled too much and boy, did my eyebrows come in for ridicule. I was devastated. I slunk off to lick my wounds. Avoided you for the rest of your visit. My fragile teenage confidence was shattered. Can you imagine my shock when it turned out I was going to have to work with you for a week? Worse, stay under the same roof.'

'Did I really say all that about you?'

'You absolutely did. You were not a pleasant young man. And Toby was even worse.' She wanted to say that she'd forgiven him. That he'd grown into a wonderful man. That we all said stupid things when we were teenagers. But she doubted he was in a mood to be receptive.

'So you were looking for revenge?'

'The thought crossed my mind. But then…'

'Then what?'

'I very quicky got to like you.'

'But you still didn't tell me. You slept with me, and you still didn't tell me.'

'That's right, because by then I didn't think it mattered,' she said, which was a fib in itself. She knew she should have told him. She didn't actually have a leg to stand on.

'This changes everything, Marissa. You're not who I thought you were.'

Her chin rose. 'Perhaps I'm not,' she said.

'I've never felt more humiliated than when Toby outed you back there.'

'I actually don't think Toby saw it that way.

He bought our story that we'd recently connected.'

'He's drunk. When he sobers up he'll realise I didn't recognise you as that girl we'd met sixteen years ago. He'll also realise you'd recognised me and wonder about that.'

'Does it matter what Toby thinks?'

'It matters that you made a fool out of me.'

'I think you're wrong, but if that's what you want to think, feel free.' She glared at him. He was right. Everything had changed. She'd been kidding herself there was something special between them. Besides, did she want to be with a man so rigid and judgemental?

'If you'll excuse me, I need to go up to my room.' She indicated what she was wearing. 'I need to get rid of Mrs Claus.'

'Go,' he said.

For a moment she almost laughed, a hysterical, non-funny kind of laugh, at the thought of them in this corridor, arguing in their Santa costumes. Thank heaven no one had seen them. It must have looked ludicrous.

As she headed for the stairs, she encountered Priya.

'That went so well,' Priya said. 'You were brilliant as Mrs Claus.'

'Thank you,' she said, barely able to string the words together.

Priya frowned. 'Are you okay?'

'Fine. But I finish up here today. I need to pack up my room and head back to London.'

'Haven't you heard? The roads are closed. We're snowed in.'

'You're joking.'

'We had some very heavy falls.'

'So I'll have to hope I can get out tomorrow.'

'Oh,' said Priya. 'We'd rather hoped you'd be staying.'

Marissa forced her voice to sound calm, businesslike. 'I'm sure I'll be back. It's been marvellous working with you. I have all fingers and toes crossed for you that you'll be taking over from Cecil when he retires.'

'I think I've got a chance,' Priya said with a smile.

'Look, I'm going to head up to my room to change. Then I need to get outside for some fresh air, before it gets dark.'

'Be quick,' Priya said.

Marissa couldn't bear to linger in Room eight for any longer than she had to. Too many memories of her and Oliver making love. She had never been happier than she had been twelve hours ago. Now she couldn't look at the bed for fear of a heart-wrenching vision of their sensuously entwined limbs.

How stupid she'd been to think she could escape the Christmas jinx—that it could have turned out any other way. What had Oliver said?

*Anything that's going to go wrong invariably goes wrong on Christmas Day.*

Another horrid thing had happened to her at Christmas. What could be worse than breaking up with him when they'd only just begun? He'd appeared so kind, so understanding. But it seemed that underneath that gentlemanly facade beat the heart of that mean-spirited, arrogant teenage boy. She'd look on this in years to come as a lucky escape. But it didn't feel like that now and she was desperately fighting tears.

She cringed at her remembered jollity. At the way she had dressed up as Mrs Claus, for heaven's sake, when she should have been Scrooge. Flirting with Oliver's Santa as Mrs Claus, letting her feelings for him show in her eyes, making no secret of where her heart lay. How could she have let her barriers down like that?

She put on jeans, a sweater, her warm puffer jacket, boots and headed back down the stairs, carrying her hat, scarf and gloves. If she didn't get outside soon, away from the central heating and the ever-present scent of pine needles, she feared another panic attack.

Thankfully, there was no wind, but it was bitterly cold outside and light snow was drifting down. Long afternoon shadows were falling across the snow-blanketed garden. It was beautiful and peaceful and being out in nature should be good for her battered soul. She stepped out onto the snow that covered the driveway and onto the grass. The snow was deep but not impossible and she set out towards the walled garden, the occasional snowflake landing lightly on her eyelashes. She would miss Longfield Manor, she would miss Edith, but most of all she'd miss Oliver.

She refused to let her thoughts go there. She'd only really known him for a week— she would as easily forget him; of course she would. Truth was, she'd first met him a lot longer than a week ago, and that teenage attraction had been like smouldering coals ready to ignite into fierce flames when she'd seen him again. She wondered if the reason she'd never had much luck with men was because she'd compared them unfavourably with her teenage heartthrob. But what about now? Would she compare every new man she met in the future to Oliver Pierce and find them lacking?

As she neared the iron gate to the walled garden, the snow started falling more heavily, until suddenly she could hardly see ahead of her. When she got to the gate, she turned back to see her footsteps had already been covered. She didn't have the world's best sense of direction, and she wasn't quite sure which was the way to turn back to the Manor. She hadn't thought to bring her phone to use the compass app, either. Don't be silly, she told herself. The walled garden is in a direct line to the house; it's still light, you'll be fine. She pushed the gate open and gasped at the beauty of the garden covered in snow. She'd just take a few moments here to contemplate her future and then go back.

How could he have spoken to Marissa the way he had? Oliver berated himself. It had been such a shock to discover that they'd met before. That this Marissa was *that* Marissa. Why on earth hadn't she reminded him? Was it because she was too nervous to, because he'd been so critical of her then? He shouldn't have called her a liar.

He'd gone back to Toby to ask him what

exactly had happened when they were sixteen, only for his old friend to confirm that
they had indeed picked Marissa's appearance
apart and had a good laugh. When Annabel
had gone off to the bathroom, Toby had con-
fessed he'd liked Marissa for himself and had
wanted to put Oliver off her by enumerating
her 'faults.' It had backfired on him, though,
as Marissa had never again come around to her
friend Samantha's house when her brother was
in residence. Toby reminded him that they'd
been private schoolboys at an all-boys school,
desperate for female company and ignorant of
what to do when they found a girl they liked.
That was no excuse, Oliver knew. He had been
keeping up with Toby, saying what he felt he
was meant to say, as good friends had been
few and far between in the hierarchical struc-
ture of his boarding school.

He had hurt Marissa, back then and just
now. He had to apologise, grovel if required.
Because he knew if he didn't, he wouldn't get
her back. And he desperately wanted her back.

Priya told him that Marissa had gone outside.

'In the snow?' he said. 'When it will be dark
soon?'

'She insisted,' Priya said. 'I'm sure she's okay.'

*But what if she wasn't?*

Fear sliced through him. What if she got lost in the snow?

*What if he'd lost her?*

Not because of the snow, but because of the way he'd treated her?

He couldn't bear it if, having found her again, he was once more without her. Because he had liked her back then, really liked her. He remembered now he'd told Granny he'd met a beautiful, friendly girl named Marissa in the midterm break when he'd visited Toby. But he'd been too shy and uncertain around girls to follow up with her. Had that name *Marissa* lodged in Granny's mind and that was why she'd made those extraordinary statements about her when Marissa had arrived at Longfield Manor. Who knew? But he did know he had to find her now, before she had time to hate him again.

There had been a light fall of snow since Marissa had set out, but not enough to completely obliterate her footsteps. He wasn't surprised to see she'd headed for the walled garden; she loved that place, felt a special bond to it.

But her footsteps were more obscured by snow when he got closer. 'Marissa!' he called. The word was loud in the silent garden blanketed by snow. He called her name again.

Then she was there at the open gate of the garden. 'Oliver. I'm here.'

He ran in the snow to the gate where she waited, all bundled up against the cold. 'Are you okay? I was worried.'

'Of course I'm okay,' she said. 'I just needed some fresh air, to clear my head after...after what happened back there.' There was a distinct chill to her voice that had nothing to do with the snow.

'Marissa, I'm sorry, so sorry for speaking to you like that. I was wrong. I was so shocked by the fact you remembered me and didn't say. But that's no excuse.'

'I was in the wrong, too,' she said. 'I should have let you vent. I had so many chances to remind you we'd met sixteen years ago but I didn't.'

'I was awful back then. Toby confirmed that we did say those horrible things you overheard. I have no excuse. I really liked you but was too shy and ignorant to know what to do about it. I wanted to keep up with Toby because he was one of the few friends I had at boarding school. My life was pretty awful in the aftermath of my parents' divorce. So even though I was uncomfortable with what he was saying, I let him egg me on. And he's stayed a good friend. Obnoxious when he's drunk, but still a loyal friend. And Annabel is a darling. He's lucky to have her.'

'You liked me then? Really?' Her eyes were huge.

'I had a funny way of showing it, didn't I?'

He explained then his theory of why the name Marissa might have triggered Granny's odd behaviour.

'It's an interesting thought,' Marissa said. 'She was right, though, wasn't she? About us being together.'

'Are we together still?'

'If you want us to be,' she said tentatively.

'Will you forgive me for my crass sixteen-year-old behaviour? Teenagers can say such stupid things, behave so badly.'

'I already have forgiven you.'

'That wasn't us back then. Fourteen-year-old you and sixteen-year-old me. They were immature, semi-formed versions of ourselves.'

'And yet, I think that's when I was struck by the *coup de foudre*. Not a week ago. Sixteen years ago.'

'You think so?'

'I know so. I have a strong feeling you have always been the man for me. We just had to find each other again.'

'And will I always be the man for you?' he said hoarsely. He held his breath for her answer.

'You always will be,' she said.

'I love you, Marissa,' he said. He had never told a woman he loved her and he was struck by how...*wonderful* it felt. 'I really love you.'

She smiled a slow, sensual smile. 'And I love you, darling Oliver.'

He kissed her and their kiss told them everything they needed to know.

'I've had a thought,' he said. 'I liked having you as my Mrs Claus and calling you my wife. How would you feel about becoming Mrs Pierce?'

'Are you proposing to me, Oliver?'

'You mean sixteen years after I first met you, I still can't find the right words to say to you?'

'Think about it. I think the right words are probably on the tip of your tongue.'

He laughed. 'Marissa Gracey, will you marry me?'

She smiled. 'I would love to marry you, Oliver Pierce, so the answer is yes.'

They kissed again, long and sweet and full of hope for their shared future.

'There are things we need to talk about,' he said. 'The future of Longfield Manor being one.'

'Is it in doubt?'

'Grandpa wanted me to sell it.'

'No! You couldn't.'

'That's the conclusion I've come to as well.'

'Good,' she said vehemently.

'I'd want you to be involved with The Pierce Group. You bring something to the table when it comes to the Manor's future as a hotel.'

'I could be the events manager. And help Edith. She'd like Priya to take over from Cecil, by the way.'

'Can we schedule in us having a family here, too?' he asked.

She smiled her delight. 'Absolutely. It'll be our top priority.'

'The women have it sorted.'

'We're good at that,' she said.

'You're good at lots of things,' he said. 'Including making me the happiest man in the world.'

'You're very good at making me the happiest woman.'

She looked up at him, her beautiful face glowing with love. 'You know you said you wanted to help me make new, happy memories of Christmas?'

'I remember.'

'I think we've just made the most wonderful

memories of Christmas, of Longfield Manor and of you. Something tells me my Grinch days are over.'

He kissed her again.

# EPILOGUE

*April the following year*

COULD THERE BE a more beautiful place for her wedding to Oliver than the Longfield Manor walled garden? Marissa didn't think so. The day was perfect, a blue sky with just a few wisps of white cloud trailing across the horizon. She stood outside the iron gate to the garden, looking in to the scene so perfectly set for the ceremony.

The fruit trees espaliered on the stone walls were blossoming in frothy bunches of white and pink, and tulips and other spring flowering bulbs lined the stone pathways. A heady, sweet scent from lily of the valley wafted through the air. Water trickled from a central fountain, at the base of which, Marissa was tickled to discover, bloomed the starry white flowers of the bogbean. The string quartet—the same one as they'd had for Christmas—played romantic, classical music.

They both wanted a simple wedding, with a celebrant from the village and an elegant lunch in one of the private rooms in the hotel. The celebrant stood at the far end of the garden, with Oliver and his best man Toby waiting for her to walk down the central pathway so they could start the ceremony. There were thirty guests, a mix of friends and family, including her brother Kevin and his wife, Danni, who had flown in from Sydney, standing and sitting around the garden. Kevin kept a firm hold on Oliver and Marissa's black Labrador puppy, Rufus Two, who was being a very good boy.

Marissa took a deep breath. She would walk down that pathway in her lovely, long white dress, her dark hair up under an exquisite veil, as Marissa Gracey, and walk back up it married to the man she adored. She could hardly wait to be his wife.

She held on tight to her bouquet and got ready to walk—she'd been told she should glide—up the pathway to where Oliver waited. First up the pathway ahead of her, in an elegant violet lace dress, was her special attendant, Edith, beaming her joy that her dream for her grandson was about to come true. Marissa had a quiet, reflective moment that her parents couldn't be here. Her mother had always wanted to see her as a bride.

Her bridesmaid Caity stepped close to her long enough to whisper with a smirk, 'I thought you were immune to gorgeous men,' before making her own way down the pathway in her slinky orchid-coloured silk satin dress. Caity's healthy, perfect twin girls were with her husband, Tom.

The quartet struck up Mendelssohn's 'Wedding March.' Then Marissa stepped onto the pathway, seeing only Oliver waiting for her, his love shining from his eyes, as she walked towards her husband-to-be and her new life with him.

*To love, honour and cherish.*

\* \* \* \* \*

*If you enjoyed this story,
check out these other great reads
from Kandy Shepherd*

Cinderella and the Tycoon Next Door
Mistletoe Magic in Tahiti
Pregnancy Shock for the Greek Billionaire
Second Chance with His Cinderella

*All available now!*